PRETTY IN THE DARK

DARK AND WILD

ANNE ROMAN

LA NOIR MEDIA, LLC

I hope you like angst, suspense, and sexy-alpha-hole bikers because this book has it. I also hope you don't hunt me down when you get to the end because that's certainly what a few of my alpha/beta readers threatened to do. It's ok though— I still love them. I'm a reader that loves twists, turns, and mic-drop moments that leave your heart racing and your mind going "W.T.F. just happened!" So there's a lot of that in this book. If you loved that in Pretty When You Lie— then you should REALLY love it in Pretty In The Dark.

This book is for 18+ readers only. You've been warned.

Possible Triggers:

Graphic sex & violence

Graphic language

Mild torture

Child abuse/sa/pornography-brief mention

Primal play

Mild D/s dynamic

Murder

Implied trafficking

Mention of drugs-unwillingly

PTSD

….and one hell of a muther-fucking cliff hanger.

But you're going to want to come back for more...

xoxo- Anne

To all those who are at home in the dark.

IN THE LAST BOOK...

Pretty When You Lie began with a tension-filled meeting between Juniper and Cade. Two young adults raised to hate each other from birth who somehow ended up falling in love, until Juniper's father convinced her to betray Cade, causing him to hate her. The heartbreak of his rejection and the guilt she felt for betraying him drove her to outrun the small town, leaving Cade behind. For five years, Juniper quietly built a life bartending in a seedy biker bar referred to as the Pit, owned by the head of the dangerous biker gang, The Diablo's. She'd never intended to return to Wild, Colorado, until one day the sheriff showed up announcing that her abusive and overbearing father was dead. Returning to Wild to raise her now orphaned brother, Juniper couldn't help but wonder if Cade had thought about her as much as she had him—

only to see that the last five years had done nothing to soften his heart toward her. In fact, he was angrier and more hate-filled than ever. Unbeknownst to Juniper, Cade had also spent the last several years away from Wild, as he'd ended up in prison for a crime that her father had framed him for. Now, after he's finally gotten his life back together and has started moving on from the tragedies of his past, he sees the one person he blames for everything. Juniper. Cade vows to get revenge, but other unexpected forces come into play, forcing them both to admit that they are still deeply attracted to each other. The tension builds until neither one of them can deny it anymore, and just when you think they are going to ride off on Cade's motorcycle into a happily ever after, a stunning discovery reveals that Juniper's former boss at the Pit is actually her half-brother, a secret society wants her for their own reasons, and Juniper's father isn't her father at all, nor is he dead.

PROLOGUE

Pale moonlight highlighted the mist that swirled through the wet grass on the garden grounds. The chilly October air made her breath come out in little puffs. Her eyes scanned the bushes and trees with their bare branches. The squeak of the garden gate made her pause, one foot half-raised to take another step on the stone path that would lead from the house to the shed.

She strained to listen for the sound of footsteps as her heartbeat thundered in her ears.

Without warning, a gloved hand covered her mouth as a powerful arm wrapped around her, pulling her into the shadows. Her eyes went wide with panic. A scream caught in her throat as she struggled.

"Shhh…shhh…Blaire, it's me." David Black's whispered voice filtered through the haze of panic and adrenaline.

His hand slipped from her mouth and she turned, her body shaking as she threw her arms around the broad shoulders of one of her oldest friends.

"Oh god, David, I have to go. He's going to kill me." Her words were whispered in terror. At any moment, the man she'd left asleep upstairs could wake and discover that she'd fled the bedroom that he had her locked in. She looked over David's shoulder at the dark, quiet Wild estate. The house's shadow cast the rest of the garden where the moonlight didn't touch, in near total darkness.

"Blaire, why are you here? You weren't supposed to be here." A glance down at his leather-gloved hands told her everything she needed to know.

"Oh my god, you're here to kill him."

David's lips pressed together in a firm line, but he didn't respond to her accusation. His eyes flicked up to the silent house, then back to her. "Niko is on his way, Blaire. You need to tell me what you were doing here. Now." There was a biting command to his tone, and it made her shift uneasily.

"I thought I could talk to him. Reason with him, but he's unhinged. Niko can't come here, David. Edmund will kill him." Her voice trailed off, fear causing her throat to close up.

"Niko is not going to leave you behind, Blaire. And I'll take care of Edmund. Now, come on. He should have the car here any minute now."

She let him lead her away but kept casting furtive glances over her shoulder, sure that she saw movement in one window. The dark house sat ominously in the night, like a brooding, disapproving figure watching her as she made her escape. A shudder went through her.

The gate squeaked again and she froze, her nails digging into the leather of David's jacket where she held on to keep from slipping on the slick stone.

She gasped, letting go of her friend when she saw the figure that stood there, not caring if she slipped as she ran toward him. "Niko!"

Thick arms wrapped themselves around her as he drew her into him. "*Sunshine…*" His voice was a gruff whisper against her hair, and she relaxed. Niko was here. "What are you doing here, my love?" He pulled back to look down at her. She knew he would be angry at her involvement, but also that he would understand. This was her mess. She needed to undo it. Only now, she saw that there was no other option. Edmund was insane.

David stepped up next to her, casting a worried frown in her direction. "She thought she could reason with him."

"He's crazy, Niko." She shook her head as the tears spilled down her face. "He wouldn't rip up the contract.

He said he'd kill me before he let anyone else have me." She drew her hand down to the front of her dress, pressing against her stomach there. "He said he didn't care that I was already carrying your baby. He just wants me..." she whispered her words in terror.

Niko's eyes darkened, the night already making them look black and soulless. "Did he touch you?" he growled the question, and she shook her head.

"No, no, Niko, I wouldn't let him. He made me stay with him and locked me in the upstairs bedroom." She gulped. She didn't tell him what else he'd said. That the minute the baby was out of her, Blaire would be Edmund Wild's completely. Whether or not she wanted it.

Some of the tension in his shoulders relaxed. "He'll not hurt you or me, *sunshine*. I promise. Come on, Kage is waiting to meet you." The moonlight glinted off his white teeth as he smiled down at her, as if her worries were nothing more than a bad dream. A dream she was more than ready to wake from. "I'm ready to meet him, too. I hope he's ready for a sister." Niko's grin widened.

"So you know it's a girl, huh?" His hand caressed her stomach, the gentlest swell of her belly the only tell that she was pregnant.

David coughed. "Niko, you need to go." Niko's eyes flew to David and he frowned.

"No. You take Blaire back to my penthouse. I'll handle this."

David shook his head. "Niko, you need to take care of Blaire and the baby now. I'll take care of Edmund."

The two men stared at each other in quiet assessment. Then Niko nodded and turned to Blaire, taking her by the hand and pulling her towards the blacked-out sedan at the end of the drive.

"You never knew when to stay in your lane, David Black."

The crisp voice pierced the night air like the crack of a whip.

All three froze in their tracks.

Blaire turned her head toward the dark shadow that was descending the front porch stairs, her eyes going wide in terror.

Edmund's ice-cold gaze met hers, and the smile that creased his thin lips reminded her of the grinning skulls. "Going somewhere, love?"

1

———

JUNIPER

"I think I just got an invitation…" I whispered the words, my hands shaking as I held the crisp, white parchment between my fingers.

The delicate scrawl of letters and numbers sent chills racing down my spine, and suddenly the delicious breakfast Cade had made for me sat like a bowling ball in my stomach. I was going to be sick, and it wasn't because of my migraine.

"An invitation to what?" I flinched at the sound of Dean's voice and quickly tucked the card back into the envelope it had come in.

"Just someone who wants to meet with me, probably for the Emporium." The lie rolled off my tongue and I felt a twinge of guilt. I was becoming too used to keeping secrets from my brother. Just like I'd become too used to keeping secrets from Cade. But Dean didn't need to know what was happening. At least not yet. Not until I could find out more about why Edmund had faked his death. And why my mother had kept me in the dark about my half-brother and my real father.

Dean's eyes narrowed in suspicion like every disbelieving pre-teen boy was prone to do at his age. He turned back to Cade. "I thought you hated her." Apparently, Cade's answer wasn't enough to satisfy his curiosity, and he wasn't going to let it go like I'd hoped he would.

My mouth gaped open in shock. "Dean!" He turned a baleful eye on me.

"What? It's true."

I watched Cade's face for a reaction, a confirmation of Dean's words—or denial. Of all the things we'd said to each other in the past several days, not once had he said he'd forgiven me. My father had pinned a crime on him he didn't commit and used me to do it. Cade had every right to want payback.

But his face gave nothing away. He just shook his head and ignored Dean like he was used to his bluntness, and instead of answering, he dropped the kitchen towel onto the counter that he'd so casually draped over his shoulder, then he turned back to me.

"I have to go, but I'll be back. Don't leave the house without telling me."

I glared at him. "I'm not under house arrest, and you're not my jailer."

A shadow passed over his face and I realized too late just how callous my words sounded. But before I could say anything else, he brushed past Dean and walked out the door. Maybe it was better this way. After overhearing his conversation with my apparent brother and realizing that the only reason Cade had been getting close to me was to keep tabs on me, I wasn't so sure I wanted to hop on the back of a bike and ride off into the sunset with him. I wasn't even sure there would be a sunset to ride off into.

Dean started to turn and walk away, but I stopped him.

"Where have you been?"

He blinked, his face going as impassive as the man who'd just walked out the door.

"Out with friends."

I frowned. "What friends? Do I know them?"

Dean's eyes narrowed, glinting with anger and stubbornness. "You're not my mom, Juniper. So why don't you stop pretending and go back to Denver? It's not like you want to be here, anyway."

I wanted to flinch at the way his sharp words slapped at me. "Dean, that's not true. I came back for you."

My hand itched with the urge to reach out and run my fingers through the sandy blonde mess of hair that curled around his eyes. Eyes that were almost the same hue as mine, with just a tad more green to them. But I kept them at my side, knowing he wouldn't appreciate the touch. "I'm sorry I wasn't here for you D. I wanted to be. You have no idea how badly I wanted to be here. But you don't understand. It was safer if I was gone."

"Well, it wasn't safe, Juniper. It wasn't safe at all." With that, Dean spun on his heel and marched down the hall to the stairs that led up to his room. The entire house shook with the sound of his door slamming and in the next instant, I heard the sounds of Bad Omen's "Concrete Jungle" thumping through the house. Bone-weary tiredness fell over me as I returned to the island counter and stared at the invitation.

I had no clue what I was doing.

Nothing was going the way I'd thought it would once I came back to Wild. It felt like someone had cursed the place. Or maybe it was just my family that was cursed.

Anger and frustration flushed through me, my skin prickling hot and then cold, and before I knew it, I snatched the envelope up and marched toward my father's study. If our family's past was involved in whatever was happening now, then I knew the answers would be in there.

I keyed in the code that would unlock the doors and pushed them open, pausing in the entryway as memories and feelings came flooding back to me. It was like taking a step back in time. Dark paneled walls gave the room an ominous feeling. Heavy curtains framed either side of a large, executive-style desk, drawn shut as if to permanently block out the sun. Edmund's presence still filled the room. I could see the couch where my brother had lain, sleeping so quietly, so peacefully, with a gun pointed at his head while I'd been kneeling on the floor, begging Edmund to spare him.

Telling him I would do anything he wanted. Anything at all. Scared to even raise my voice above a whisper for fear of waking Dean.

I bit my lip and tore my gaze away from the couch to the fireplace, lying cold and dark now. But it had blazed brightly during the cold, winter nights. And often during the summer as well.

If I breathed deeply enough, I could almost smell the scent of his favorite cigar and see him sitting in front of the fireplace in his leather chair, watching the flames.

He'd done that more and more as I got older. Watched the flames, and sometimes when he thought I wasn't paying attention, I could feel him watching me. Observing me. His eyes glinting with thoughts I didn't want to know.

Once when I'd been planting new herbs in our garden for Bess, I'd caught him staring at me over the fence. And when I'd asked him if everything was okay, he'd just approached me as if in a trance, lifting a lock of my hair and letting it slide between his fingers. His voice had whispered my mother's name like a prayer. *"Blaire..."* Then whatever memory he'd been lost in slipped away, and he'd come back to the present with a cold sneer on his lips. A look I was more familiar with. "You're so much like your mother."

It wasn't a compliment.

Chills ran down my spine at the memory. Had Edmund realized then that I wasn't his daughter? What had he done to my mother when he'd found out?

I moved toward the large, cherry wood desk that sat in the center of the room. It was ornate and still had papers and notes organized on top of it, as if Edmund had gotten up in the middle of a task and walked away, never to return.

When the solicitor had been here to handle the reading of the will and deal with the remains of the estate, I hadn't paid any attention to what had been on the desk. But now I did.

Notes from a case he'd been working on. Phone numbers and names to other attorneys. Some of them I recognized as colleagues he spoke about. I ignored all of those and pulled open the drawers.

They were filled with organized file folders and documents, most of them to do with the house or various businesses he'd been interested in at one point.

One file caught my attention. It was labeled with just two initials, D.B. My heart clenched as I pulled it free and realized it was the bank documents from David Black's business loan. I flipped through the pages and gasped. No, it was more than that. It was David's entire criminal history.

As I scanned through the records, one particular arrest caught my attention. A date just a few months before my birth. They had arrested David for criminal trespassing. But it was *where* that shocked me. This house. My home.

I scanned through the remains of the report, but all it stated was that they apprehended David for breaking and entering with another accomplice, who was shot and killed in self-defense. They had redacted the name of the person who David had been with, as well as the name of the person who had shot him.

Could this have been the cause of the hatred Edmund felt toward Cade's family? Edmund had never really told me why he hated the Blacks so much. He'd only ridiculed them for their lack of class and made them out to be the worst of enemies. I set the file aside to think about later.

Everything else was boring and mundane. Nothing that would have given me any sign that he had been planning to fake his death, or the reason why.

Frustrated with how little I knew, I shoved the chair away and then winced in pain as my knee banged hard against the underside of the desk. Rubbing the sore spot, I glared at the offending drawer and then felt a small thrill as something caught my eye. The placement of the drawer didn't match up with where my knee hit.

Frowning, I ran my fingers along the underside of the wood until something caught my fingernail.. "Come on baby…" I coaxed, until my nail slid in between the sliver of space and a grin spread across my face. A false bottom!

Excitement built as I emptied the contents of the drawer, searching for the release that would open the secret compartment. With a slight gasp, I felt the drawer give way. Carefully reaching inside the tiny space, I felt around until I pulled out a few faded pictures, my heart clenching as I realized they were of my mother.

But not just my mother.

Edmund was there too. They weren't together, however. Between the two of them, there were two other men. One of them surprised me. David Black, Cade's father, was grinning from ear to ear with his arm slung around Edmund's shoulders as though they were close friends.

And my mother was gripping the arm of another man. Her head leaned against his shoulder as if she was melting into him. There was a soft, secretive smile playing around her lips.

I studied the face of the unknown man, not recognizing him and yet, feeling as if he was so familiar somehow. His hair was dark and long, pulled back in a ponytail. Despite the faded photo, it appeared that he had dark eyes and a dark complexion.

I glanced over Edmund's face again and noticed that he was the only one not smiling in the photo. Instead, his head was tilted away from the camera and his gaze was fixed on my mother. There was an intensity in the way he was looking at her that made me shiver. I recognized that look.

Setting the photos down, I felt around again for anything else, until my fingers touched the edge of something that seemed to be caught in the back. Giving it a tug, I felt it snap as I pulled free a tarnished silver necklace, with a key dangling from the end. I held the key up to the light and frowned.

Pushing away from the desk, I stood and did a slow circle around the room, as if something might jump out at me and scream, "Here I am! I'm the secret your mom and family have been hiding all these years. So glad you found me!"

But the bookcases were silent, with only a thick coat of dust blanketing them. The fireplace just looked cold, and it was filled with dark ashes. I looked at the tiny key in my hand for clues, but nothing about it stood out to me, and I gritted my teeth in frustration. I was close to finding out something—I could feel it. And yet, the truth was still just out of my reach. The dull thud of my headache came back to me, pounding against my temple as frustration and exhaustion took over.

I was so tired of feeling like I was alone and in the dark.

2

JUNIPER

The buzz of my tattoo gun filled the shop, accompanied by the occasional grunt of pain from the large man in my chair with his shirtless back exposed to me. I lifted my gun, dipping it in more ink. The tattoo could have been finished half an hour ago if the giant baby—who kept his eyes squeezed shut the entire time, had stayed still and stopped squirming.

"John, sit still. I swear you're acting like you've never done this before."

He gave me another grunt and opened his eyes. "Well, you're practically on my damn spine!"

The shop door jingled, but I didn't look up to see the customer who walked in. "Be with you in a minute!" I called out.

Bending my head back to my work, I finished the delicate outline of a tiny robin hiding within the tree boughs. Whoever this new girlfriend of John's was, I hope she knew how lucky she was. I also hoped she'd be the last. He was running out of available skin to get the name tattooed of every new girl he fell in love with.

The branches of the tree dipped and swirled almost as if by chaotic design. But it was all an illusion. Her name was there within the bend of a branch, the shading of leaves, the twist of a vine. For being a cover-up and a name, it was some of my best work. I couldn't help but smile and admire it. John had better not get his heart broken by this one.

John left, and I pulled off my mask and gloves as I approached the woman who was standing in my waiting area with a smile. She was pretty, a little older than I was, with silvery blonde hair and wide, baby-blue eyes. There was a pinched look around her eyes and a nervousness in her gaze that made me think she might be a first-timer.

"Hey! If you're looking for custom work, I'm booked solid for the next two months." Even saying that felt surreal. In the last few weeks since the Emporium had opened, I'd been flooded with custom requests and tattoo bookings. It was to the point where I'd wondered if I might need to hire outside help. And it hadn't only been my shop, the entire Emporium had been flooded with business. So much so that I'd barely seen Vy, Lacey or any of the other ladies. "But if you want some quick flash, you can pick one of the pieces from my book on the coffee table." I nodded to an old table I'd pulled from a garage sale a few days ago, it displayed some of my custom flash pieces.

The woman shook her head and offered me a shy smile. "Thank you, no. I'm not here for a tattoo. I'm actually here to talk about the Wild One's Foundation. Are you Juniper?"

Understanding dawned. She wasn't nervous about a tattoo. She was here to seek help. That was another development over the past week. After announcing the foundation and its mission, we received an overwhelming number of calls from women and other organizations inquiring about what we could offer them. The only problem was, that it had been hard to get them the help that they so desperately needed. The bureaucratic red tape surrounding the acquisition of the land and building for the foundation's shelter, was so extensive that not even my last name could expedite the process. It had been frustrating for all of us.

I felt my heart sink a little as I took in the woman's hopeful expression, noting the dark circles under her eyes. She needed our help. I just didn't know if we could provide it yet.

"That's me." I held out my hand, and she took it.

"Leia." She said, and I noticed there was a determination in her grip and her gaze. No matter what limited resources we had, I knew the one thing that could always help was a listening ear. My stomach rumbled. I needed a break and maybe a snack. An idea dawned.

"Do you like brownies?"

Leia gave me a confused look. "Well, yes…" she trailed off and watched me in confusion as I switched off the lights and flipped my sign from *open* to *closed*.

"Well, come on then. My friend Vy makes the best death-by-chocolate brownies, and I know the look of a woman who needs a good brownie when I see one."

"I'm sorry. What does this have to do with the Wild One's Foundation?" She asked, as I opened the door and motioned for her to exit.

"Everything. You'll see."

We made our way down the faux cobblestone street and I waved to a few vendors who were tidying up outside their shops. Here in the emporium, it was like the outside world didn't exist. Every time I opened its doors and stepped inside, my problems slipped to the back of my mind and for a little while, I could forget. Seeing the women who ran the shops, working on my art or pieces for my clients, knowing that everything we did here was for something greater, made it all disappear. For a while, at least.

Until I went home and stood in the dim interior of my father's study, hunting for whatever the key that I found would unlock.

Dean and Bess thought I was crazy. They didn't say it, but I could see the look in their eyes every time they walked past the open door and found me knocking on panels, pushing on bricks, or pulling down all the books on the shelves. Not that Dean talked to me, anyway. After the argument we'd gotten into the other day, he'd gone back to being silent and sulky. I'd tried to talk to him once again this morning before I left for work, reminding him we had a meeting with the principal today, but all I'd gotten out of him was a short. "Fine."

Cade hadn't been much better. For all his talk about not going anywhere, he'd been silent as a ghost, only asking me if I had found the picture I'd mentioned to him, but when I told him I couldn't find the old photo album anymore, he'd just grunted and hung up. Part of me couldn't help but feel the hurt of his absence. His words from our night together and the way he'd made my body come apart at the seams, still played on an endless loop in my mind. But then, so did the conversation I'd overheard. A conversation I wasn't meant to hear and one he'd never apologized for. I wasn't so sure that his silence wasn't for the best.

One night of amazing, mind-blowing, best sex I'd ever

had, did not make up for years of lies and hurt. I bit my lip, worrying it between my teeth as we approached Vy's bakery. Especially considering the things he'd confessed he'd experienced at my father's hands after I'd left. All because I'd been forced to choose between him and my brother. All because the lie had been easier than the truth.

The smell of chocolate and sugar hit my senses as I push open the door and beckon Leia to follow. Warm, brown eyes greeted me as one of my oldest friends looked up from the counter where she was icing cupcakes, and I smiled. Leia wasn't the only one in need of one of Vy's famous brownies. My own heart could use a little chocolate remedy as well.

A couple of hours later, Leia left with a bright smile and a visible weight lifted off her thin shoulders. A weightlessness that all of us, Lacey, Vy and myself, felt as well. Finally, something was going right for us and the Wild One's Foundation.

Lacey would call it fate, or manifestation, or whatever spiritual mumbo-jumbo she'd learned from some great granny of hers. I wasn't sure what divine force, if any, influenced the sequence of events that led Leia Morrow to our door, but I was grateful.

After finding out that she'd been a successful marketing director of a large corporation, and hearing her heartbreaking story of loss, we knew she'd be the perfect person to pitch our dream to the powers that be, moving it beyond an idea and into a full-fledged organization. The idea that not only would she be helping us, but we'd be helping her out of her shit situation, also attributed to the lightness in my step. A lightness that I carried with me all the way to the middle school parking lot where I sat inside my car and steeled myself for the meeting that was to come.

3

JUNIPER

The principal had been kind and understanding on the phone when I'd finally called her back to schedule the meeting. We'd agreed that we both wanted what was best for Dean, and so this meeting was to sit down and plan the best course of action. A plan I desperately hoped would not only steer Dean onto the right path, but keep him safe as well. I knew one thing, however, nothing was going to happen if Dean, himself, wasn't on board with it. And so far, he had been resistant to anything I'd tried to implement or suggest.

I still hadn't said anything to Dean about Edmund being alive and in hiding, but I knew I was going to have to break it to him sooner or later. Hopefully, this new brother I had yet to meet, would have some answers for me. Frustration had me slamming my car door shut harder than I meant to, causing a few of the students that were still hanging out in the parking lot to look in my direction. They took one look at my dingy, yellow VW bug, with the red skull still grinning from the hood, and snickered.

I cringed. I still hadn't gotten the skull removed or the hood repainted. When the ladies at the Emporium had asked about it, I'd brushed it off as kids playing pranks. Which may or may not still be true. Part of me hoped that I'd get a phone call from the sheriff's office and be told that they'd discovered a gang of kids trying to stir up trouble, and all of this would be a lesson in teenage boredom.

A sudden thought struck me. The sheriff was the one who told me about my dad's death when he'd found me in Denver. He had to have information or know *something* that would help me solve the mystery. I remembered the file I'd found in Edmund's office filled with David Black's criminal history. I decided it was time to visit the *honorable* sheriff. The thought made my stomach roll. The sheriff wasn't exactly on my list of favorite people considering his relationship with Edmund, and I was reluctant to have anything to do with him. But there were too many questions that needed answering, and other than my mysterious missing brother, he was the only person I knew who might have actual information. I just didn't want to know what the price of that information would be.

By the time I'd decided on my next course of action, I was in the school office and waiting for the principal to get done with the meeting before mine. Dean was already there, a sullen look on his face as if he'd had one too many experiences inside these walls. Guilt twisted my heart again. I'd thought by leaving I was protecting my little brother. But it seems all I'd done was make things worse for everyone. I needed to come up with a way to prove to Dean that he could trust me, and that I wasn't going anywhere, ever again.

The door to the principal's office opened and I straightened, suddenly nervous. This was my first opportunity to show Dean that I was serious about my role as his guardian. I couldn't fuck this up.

A short woman with jet-black hair, streaked with a few wisps of silver, pulled back into a neat chignon with dark eyes that sparkled with kindness, greeted us.

"Ms. Wild! So glad you could come in today." She turned to Dean, her smile softening. "And Dean, I'm glad to see you again."

I blinked in confusion. For the way that Dean had sulked and balked at coming to meet the principal, I'd expected her to be a half-monster. But this woman gave me the impression that she'd rather hand you a cup of tea and a muffin than dole out a punishment.

We sat down across from her desk, both of us shifting with nervous tension in our seats.

The principal broke the awkward silence. "First, I wanted to express my condolences over the passing of your father, Ms. Wild." She gave me a sympathetic look, and it was all I could do to not cringe and blurt out, "No need. He's not dead, just a deadbeat dad. Ha!" But I knew that wouldn't go over well. Instead, I gave her a tight-lipped smile and nodded, hoping she wouldn't elaborate or talk about what a paradigm he was in the community.

"I know this has been a difficult transition for both you and Dean, but I'm hoping this plan will help redirect his energies in a more positive manner, and help develop that already brilliant mind." I smiled and nodded again. This wasn't anything that we hadn't already discussed together and I knew that the principal was reiterating what we'd talked about for Dean's benefit, not mine.

"Dean, your sister said she's spoken to you about what we are proposing and that you are open to the idea. Is this true?" She looked directly at Dean now, and although she presented it as if he had a choice in the matter, he didn't. Either Dean had to get on board with the plan, or they would suspend him and send him to an alternative school. Luckily, Dean was more than excited about the opportunity and, for the first time in a long time, I saw a spark of his old, boyish excitement peeking through. "Yeah, it sounds a hell of a lot better than this stupid place."

I bit my tongue to keep from snapping at him to watch his language. But she just took it in stride and gave him a wide smile. "Great! I'm so glad you agree! This academy is the first of its kind in the state. But it's received some amazing accolades already and is touted as one of the best academies in the entire country. You'll get some hands-on experience while working on your education. Plus, grants and a scholarship from a local benefactor completely paid for all the living costs." She said the last part to me as she folded her hands on her desk and leaned forward, a twinkle in her eye. "And make no mistake, Dean, this was not an easy program to get you into. Be on your absolute best behavior there or you *will* be expelled. And I'm afraid there won't be much else I, or anyone else, can do for you after that."

I frowned. "And you're sure this place is safe?"

Dean's new school was in another city a couple of hours from Wild. I had struggled hard with the idea of sending him so far away, worried that he'd view it as me—once again, abandoning him. Or pushing him off on someone else. But when I'd shown him the pamphlet and told him I wouldn't even consider it, that we'd find something else, he'd shocked me by asking if I'd ever considered what *he* might want? And then he'd shoved the pamphlet in his pocket and said anything was better than sticking around here. I thought he was just being a disgruntled teen, but since that day, I'd caught him looking at the pamphlet several times, and had even overheard him excitedly pointing out all the extra-curricular programs to Bess when he didn't realize I was listening.

She graced me with an emphatic smile. "The children of some of the state's most influential families attend Mountainside Academy, including the governor's own son. I assure you they take their security very seriously."

Mountainside Academy for Distinguished Studies. It was a mouthful to say, and exactly what it sounded like. A public preparatory school for those who wished to push themselves beyond the usual, public academic standards. Supposedly, anyone in the state could apply and get accepted so long as they met their scholastic and testing guidelines, with grants and public funding available for those who couldn't afford the tuition and living costs.

I didn't know what strings the principal had pulled to get Dean to be considered for the program since it was already well into the school year, and we'd missed the deadline to apply for scholarships. But I was beyond thankful for her connections.

I returned her smile. "Thank you so much, ma'am. We genuinely appreciate all you've done. Are you sure you can't tell me who the benefactor was that covered Dean's living expenses? I'd love to thank them in person."

Her smile stretched wider. "Of course! Actually, I went ahead and asked if he'd mind stopping by to lend his support, just in case Dean, or yourself, needed some extra reassurance." She reached across her desk and hit the call button for her secretary. "Alice, please send Mr. Black in now."

4

JUNIPER

Several emotions went through me all at once. Surprise. Anger. And the tingling awareness of Cade that was always present whenever he was near.

The last emotion I shoved down deep behind the others, glaring at his tall figure as he framed the doorway. A leather jacket clung to his shoulders, breaking open just enough that I could see the dark shirt he wore underneath stretching across his chest, highlighting the muscles that bunched as he moved. Hazel eyes flecked with gold pierced through mine, as though he knew every thought and emotion I was feeling at that exact moment. My teeth ground together so hard that my jaw hurt. He didn't even have the decency to look sheepish or apologetic for springing this surprise on me.

I turned back to the principal. "Absolutely not."

Her brows shot up in surprise. "I'm sorry, Juniper, is there a problem?"

I leaned forward, my words coming out short and clipped as I fought to maintain composure. "Hell yeah there's a fucking problem." The principal gasped slightly at my language and the sudden change in my attitude. "The problem is, that you didn't tell me that *he—*" my finger pointed in accusation at Cade, who'd just shut the door behind him, leaning against it with thick arms crossed over his chest and a dark smirk playing across his lips. "...was the *mysterious benefactor.*" I air-quoted with a side-eyed look of disgust in Cade's direction. He only gave me a stony, blank-faced response back.

Her confused gaze flicked between me and Cade with a small frown. "I see." She said slowly, drawing out the words as if she was trying to take the time to piece together the unknown facts, but couldn't quite make it add up.

"Unfortunately, Juniper, without Mr. Black's generous donation to the scholarship, the living expenses would have to be paid out of pocket by you." She tried to smile and compose herself. "I'm assuming that won't be an issue?"

My smile was tight. It would sure as hell be a fucking

issue. A major one, considering the lack of zeros at the end of my bank statement. "Of course not. How much are the estimated costs?"

She opened up a file and pulled out a spreadsheet. "According to the Academy, estimated living expenses for student residents are on average five thousand dollars…" I perked up. That number wasn't so bad. I could scrounge up enough money, maybe even sell a few custom art pieces, and Dean could still attend the school. "…Per month."

My jaw dropped. "Excuse me? Did you say five thousand dollars *per month*?!"

She reached across her desk to hand me the sheet so I could see the number for myself. "Yes, that covers the cost of food, amenities, residency, and any extracurricular expenditures the students may require."

"Where are they taking these kids to, France?" My eyes grew wider, my stomach sinking as the number of dollars and cents grew larger the further down I read on the column of listed expenses.

"Why, yes! Actually, there are opportunities for student exchange programs, if that's something that Dean is interested in."

"I don't know—I can't—" Spots danced in my vision as my rage built up.

"Juniper, if Dean doesn't go to this school, the only other option is transferring him to the alternative school. I know you don't want that." Her voice was kind, but firm. The school board wouldn't back down on this.

My hands were well and truly tied. I had to choose between Dean going to this fancy-pants school, and Cade once again coming in to save my ass with a monetary donation, or letting my brother go to the *alternative school*. I opened my mouth to ask if there were any other reasonable options, but I caught Dean staring at me out of the corner of my eye, and I snapped it shut. He hadn't said a word, but I could see the tension coiled in his shoulders, his eyes a mixture of excitement and worry as they darted between me and Cade. And hope. Hope that I would say yes. Hope that I won't shut this down and tell him no. Hope that Cade could somehow change my mind.

I could see it then. The bond between them. I might not like it, but I couldn't deny it any more than I could deny the tension and energy that I felt between me and Cade the moment he walked into the room.

I sighed, resigned to my situation. "Fine. We—graciously..." I snuck a glance at Cade, who'd remained a silent sentinel during the entire conversation. "...accept this scholarship." Dean's grin was blinding as he let out an exaggerated, "Let's go!"

'However—," I held up my hand and looked between

the principal and Dean, refusing to give any more attention to Cade. What I was doing was for Dean's benefit, not Cade's. And I was still furious that he hadn't discussed this with me first. "I'm not saying this is forever, either. If we can find another scholarship or way to pay, I'd like the option to look into it."

Dean looked like he was about to argue, but swallowed whatever he was going to say when Cade cleared his throat in warning. Instead, he just dipped his head and mumbled a rough, "Thanks, Juniper."

My heart warmed. It was the first nice thing Dean had said to me since I'd returned to Wild. Maybe this was the start of us rebuilding the relationship that we'd lost. Hope bloomed.

"Great!" The principal stood, grinning. "I'm sure you all have a lot to discuss. We will meet again in a month to talk about Dean's progress and any concerns that come up."

Dismissed, we left the office and made our way to the entrance. I did my best to speed walk as fast as I could to avoid the heavy presence of the man at my back. Until I was sure I wasn't within earshot of any teachers or students, I didn't want to risk unleashing my temper on the overbearing asshat.

I made it to my car in the parking lot when a dark shadow fell over me.

"Going somewhere, pretty girl?"

I stiffened at the rumbling voice in my ear, glancing up to see Dean watching us with narrowed eyes.

"Yeah, home. Not that it's any of your business." I opened my car door and made to get in, but was stopped with a hand on my arm.

"Wrong. It's always my business." He pulled me away from the door and shut it. "We need to talk."

"What could you possibly want to talk about, Cade?" Sarcasm dripped from my voice as I pulled my arm out of his grasp, glaring at him. Damn the sun for being just behind his tall figure, wreathing him in dark shadows that kissed his skin and turned his hazel eyes more green than gold. "Oh, like maybe the fact that you went behind my back and so generously paid for Dean's school without even discussing it with me? Do you think that just throwing your money in my face will make your problems go away? Make *me* go away?" I tipped my chin up as he studied me, his face an impassive mask.

Dean grunted, giving us a disgusted glare. "Really? You guys are going to do this *here*?" We both turned to look at him and he just shook his head. "I'm going to the library to study. Pick me up when you're done." Then he turned away, with his hands shoved in his pockets and his hoodie pulled low over his face as he stalked off, in that teenage way of saying, *I'm too cool to care.* I watched to make sure he was heading in the direction of the library, waiting until he disappeared between the double doors before I turned back to Cade. The asshole didn't even have the decency to look apologetic.

"I didn't call the principal. Jessica called *me*."

I snorted. "And of course we're on a first-name basis with her. I don't care how it was done, Cade. You could have given me the respect I deserve as Dean's sister by asking if I even wanted help! I am his guardian, not you!"

Cade's jaw clenched, revealing his frustration. "And where were you when Dean was coming into my shop, beaten and bloodied by the idiot kids at school who thought it was cool to pick on the Wild boy?"

He took a step closer pitching his voice low. "Where were you when he was left by himself for days on end, with only your housekeeper around?" he asked. "No friends. No dad. No *sister*. No one cared about him or what he was getting himself involved with."

Guilt cut through me, sharper than a knife. How many times had I thought the same thing?

"That's right. While some of us were trapped in prisons, *you* were out there living it up in your new found freedom. And I'm not talking about the place where they sent me to be locked up. I'm talking about the hell Dean had to go through when your dad realized you weren't coming back. So if you want to know why your brother turns to me, or why the principal calls *me*, you need to think beyond what some piece of paper says you are to Dean. Or you're nothing more than just another version of Edmund Wild. Controlling Dean and his life simply because you *can*, not because you care."

My stomach knotted. When I left, I never thought that Dean would be at the mercy of a monster, I thought I was saving him. But what Cade was accusing me of now was completely wrong. I didn't want to control Dean's life. I just wanted better for him.

"I'm not trying to control Dean at all. I left to *protect* him." I hissed. "Don't you think it killed me being away from my brother? I hated every minute. But there was nothing I could do. The second I came back, Edmund would have used him against me. Dean was never safe so long as I was here. Leaving was the only option I had." I spread my arms, pleading.

"Cade, I know I hurt you and others by leaving. But did you ever consider how much leaving hurt *me?*"

He shook his head. "No, you don't get off the hook for this. I understand why you did what you did to me. Our families have been at each other's throats for so long that I should have expected it. I can't say I'm ready to forgive you yet, but I know what it's like to be forced to become someone you never wanted to be." He tipped his chin in Dean's direction. "But in Dean's eyes, you abandoned him, and now you have the audacity to come back and think he's just going to listen to you?"

Sighing, I folded my arms, looking up at the cold mountains which surrounded our city. No matter where you were in Wild, the mountains loomed in the background. Most days, I found their ancient presence comforting, protective even. Other days, they just reminded me that I was trapped by the choices other people had made. The air was heavy with the scent of snow. It wouldn't be long before we'd get our first dusting and the mountain passes would be too hard to get through, leaving only the main highway accessible. And if it was a harsh winter? Even that would get shut down and we'd be well and truly trapped until the snowplows could dig us out.

Welcome to Wild, where even modernization and the 21st century couldn't halt mother nature if she decided to be a bitch.

"You're right."

He cocked his head, those dazzling hazel eyes bearing into my soul, and I shifted uneasily against the cold metal of my car door.

"It was stupid of me to come back and think that things could go back to the way they were when I left. I just…" I looked up at the mountains again. Was Edmund up there somewhere? Was he watching me even now? My eyes darted towards the doors Dean had disappeared through. Was he watching Dean?

"Hoped," Cade finished for me, and I glanced back at him, seeing that his expression had softened a bit. I nodded.

"Yeah. I'd hoped."

5

CADE

I wanted to take back my words. They may have had a ring of truth in them, but they were harsh, and I could see the guilt she carried all over her face. But the minute she'd told me it was none of my business, I couldn't help myself. Everything about her was my business, whether or not I wanted it to be.

That seemed to be the recurring problem I had whenever she was near. Everything I meant or didn't mean to do, went right out the window. Which was why after I'd left her house a few days ago, I'd stayed away despite telling her I wouldn't.

It was for her own good. Or so I kept telling myself.

And what she didn't know was that it had been my suggestion to send Dean to the prep school. Not because I didn't feel it was the best place for him, but because I knew that as long as Dean was around, Juniper would be more worried about his safety than her own. And to be honest, I was worried about it too. Dean had gotten too used to being left to his own devices to stay put when he was told. Not to mention, there had been hard evidence that whoever was fucking with Juniper, was also taking an interest in her brother. I couldn't let Dean get sucked into this life. Not if there was anything I could do about it.

I hadn't grown up with a family other than the rough bikers my father brought around, and Kage was the only other kid. I'd never had a mother. She'd left when I was just a baby and my father had never had any other children after me. He had said the life he led was too hard on a family. And it was, but it didn't mean that as a kid I hadn't wondered what it would be like to grow up with one. A mom, a dad who didn't lose himself in blackouts and drunken rages, and maybe even a brother.

I'd seen the same sort of loneliness in Dean when he'd begun hanging around the shop. The kind of loneliness that would end with him going down a dark road. One that I'd barely escaped from, if you could even call my on-again-off-again partnership with Kage an escape. Sending him to the alternative school would be the first of many steps toward that future, and I'd do everything in my power to prevent it if I could.

Even if that meant going behind Juniper's back and wounding her pride.

When I realized the silence had dragged on and Juniper was staring off into the mountains, lost in her thoughts, I cleared my throat and she swung her clear, blue eyes back to me. There was a shadow to them, I recognized. The shadow of memories and secrets that haunted her. Secrets that were still painted on the hood of her car. Secrets I was even now trying to uncover without her knowing it, so that I could spare her more of her father's influence. The meeting Kage had set up had gotten postponed, as he'd had to deal with some internal business, but as soon as he got back into the city, we'd be sitting down to discuss the plan. And the only plan I cared about? Was killing Edmund Wild before he could make Juniper's life even more of a mess than he already had.

"Have you decided what you're going to do?"

Wariness entered her gaze. "I don't know what you mean."

She was being cagey again. Cautious. Fuck that.

"Don't start playing the game now, pretty girl. You know you won't win. What are you going to do about the invitation?"

She huffed and hugged herself tighter. The air was getting chilly as the sun was setting behind the mountains. I thought she was going to ignore me or deflect again, instead; she looked back up at the darkening peaks in the distance. "I don't know. Nothing makes sense."

Truth.

I could hear it in her voice.

Uncertainty and truth.

Maybe I was an ass for staying away. This wasn't the same Juniper that had been forced to betray me so that she could earn her father's favor and spare her brother's life.

"Can Bess come pick up Dean?" I asked, before I could talk myself out of it.

A golden brow arched at me in question. "Maybe. I don't like leaving him by himself for long, though. Why?"

I smirked, enjoying the confusion I saw in her eyes and the way her tongue darted out to lick her lips in nervousness, as I pressed in closer.

"That's for me to know and you to find out." I found my fingers reaching up to brush an errant lock of golden-blonde hair out of her eyes. "Do you trust me?"

A memory came back like a movie scene playing out in real life. The first time I'd asked her out on a date and had picked her up outside of Katie's diner on my dad's old, late-model Harley 'Fat Boy'. The bike had been almost more than I could handle, heavy, with ape hanger handlebars that I could barely reach. She'd been dressed in an all-white sundress with a string of pearls around her neck that had bobbed with every excited movement she made.

"Do you trust me?" Nervous sweat had lined my palms, and I felt them slip on the slick metal of the handlebars as I held a hand out to her. Could she tell? Could she tell this was the first time I'd ever done anything like this?

Her twin pools of blue, like deep mountain lakes, studied both me and the massive bike for a moment before she'd nodded with a shy smile, and placed her hand in mine. "I trust you." A feeling I'd never experienced before had flooded through me. I felt like I could fly. Like I could walk through steel walls. Like I could do anything. All for her. All because of her and those three simple words. I'd pulled her onto the bike behind me and she'd screamed with joy as we'd roared out of the city. Her small, delicate hands had wrapped around my waist, her body pressing against me, and as the blacktop rolled beneath us, Wild disappeared behind us. For the first time, I'd finally understood what it meant to be happy. To be free.

Her breath caught as she studied me. Maybe she was remembering the same thing I was, because with a soft voice, she shook her head. "Yes. I probably shouldn't, but I still trust you, Cade."

An anxiousness I hadn't realized I was holding onto, released. "Good. Get Dean a ride and meet me at the old football field."

Twenty minutes later, I was standing under the

bleachers on the fifty-yard line of what used to be the high school football field, but now was only used for conditioning and practice. It was empty except for a few crows that were fighting over an errant lunch some kid had left behind. I saw Juniper approach and waited until she'd almost passed my hiding spot, before I reached out and pulled her into the shadows of the bleachers with me. She yelped, and managed to land a solid punch into my gut. It didn't hurt, but I was impressed.

"Who taught you to punch like that, pretty girl?"

She shook her hand out and glared at me. "Jesus, Cade! What the hell are you doing? Are you trying to scare me? I thought you wanted to show me something."

"I do. Now answer the question. Who taught you to punch like that?" I leaned against one of the metal supports and waited for her to answer. The sun had almost completely settled behind the mountains now, and the evening's twilight cast a deeper shadow on the bleachers than the rest of the field. Unless someone walked right up to us, we were completely hidden from most of the world.

She huffed, flexing her hand. "Not that it's any of your business, but an ex-boyfriend. It was about the only thing he was good for."

Instant black rage settled over my vision at the mention of another man touching her, teaching her, even being near her. But I reined it in. The way she spoke made it sound like it hadn't been a long-standing relationship, anyway.

"Why would he need to teach you how to punch?" A needling worry flickered through my thoughts. I had no clue what Juniper had gone through once she'd left Wild. In my mind, she'd left and moved on with her life. I'd never considered the kind of life she'd led. But then I remembered Kage had mentioned that she'd worked for him at one point, and suddenly I realized I didn't know much about the Juniper that was standing in front of me now.

"Because he had a bad habit of getting us into situations that I needed to be able to punch my way out of. That's what I get for dating on the biker scene." She shrugged as if it wasn't a big deal. As if she hadn't just told me she'd been put in dangerous situations by someone who should have been protecting her. By someone like me.

I snarled. "What's his name?"

She blinked in surprise at my reaction, and then snorted. "Oh please. Are you seriously jealous? Mr. has-his-own-online-fan-club-of-fender-bunnies just waiting to jump on for a ride?"

The image of the sweet and shy Juniper from before, faded into the distance. Whatever had happened, that version of her was gone, and in front of me was a woman who wasn't afraid to go toe-to-toe with me, or call me out on my shit.

A grin curled at the corner of my lips as I stalked toward her, secretly pleased that she stood her ground and didn't back away from me. "I don't get jealous, pretty girl. I don't need to when I know that while he may have taught you how to throw a semi-decent punch, he could never have made you scream around his cock like I can." I grabbed the hand she'd punched me with and held it up, bending her fingers until they formed a solid wall and tucking her thumb into position. "But it sure sounds like you do. Next time, keep your elbow in tight to your body and power through your hip. If you ever need to punch your way out of a situation, then it had better be a punch that counts."

She stared at me, mouth gaped open slightly before her jaw snapped shut. And then the next thing I knew, I was doubled over and gasping for air.

She'd just fucking punched me. Really punched me. And now she was standing over me with a gloating grin spreading across those beautiful lips.

I forgot the reason I'd asked her to meet me here. Forgot the apology that I'd wanted to give her, or the reminder of what we'd once been together. Of the sweet kiss we'd shared here and the promise that was still etched in the metal frame of the bleachers we were standing under.

This Juniper was something new, something different. There was a darkness in her that I'd never seen before, and damn if it didn't appeal to the darkness inside of me. It made me want to test it, to push the boundaries and see how far she'd go. How far she'd let me go.

I stood up to my full height. "Most men who punch me don't get a second opportunity." Her nostrils flared-out and her breathing hitched as I move in closer, crowding her space and senses. Fuck, she looked so tiny when I towered over her like this. Her head tipped back to take me in and I had to curl my hands at my side to keep from wrapping the blonde lengths of her hair in my fist to yank it back further.

"Well, it's a good thing I'm not a man." Her voice was a seductive purr that had my balls tightening with need.

"No, you're not. I'd destroy a man that sucker-punched me like that, pretty girl. Any ideas on what I should do to you?"

A pink tongue darted out to wet her lips, and I watched, transfixed by her every move. "What do you think you can do to me that you haven't already, Cade Black?"

I chuckled darkly. "Oh, there's so much more. But if I were you, I'd run, pretty girl."

Don't run. Don't run, Juniper. I will catch you.

I leaned down just enough to catch the honey and lavender scent that was uniquely Juniper, my nose barely grazing against her hair. "But be sure that's absolutely what you want, Juniper Wild. Because when I catch you, I'm going to punish you. Do you understand?"

Her eyes danced in the dimness, shining brightly as her mouth popped open with a soft gasp. "Oh, shit…" she breathed, as if she just realized what she'd done. She took a step back. *Don't do it, pretty girl.*

Her shoes crunched on the gravel. *Fuck.*

She ran.

6

JUNIPER

I ran.

The way he'd looked at me. His eyes had darkened and his lip curled in a half snarl as he dared me to run, dared me to escape him.

It had been like a command my body had no choice but to obey.

My Converse sneakers skidded on the loose gravel as I scrambled through the metal framing that held up the risers of the old bleachers.

It had only taken me a moment to remember this exact place. The way I'd teased and taunted him until he'd finally given in and kissed me.

The way he'd pushed me away when I'd wanted to go farther and he'd said no.

He'd always said no when I so desperately wanted him

to say yes. And then he'd carved our initials in the metal frame and told me it was a promise.

I ducked under a low, metal bar, my heart racing as I took a moment to look over my shoulder, my eyes searching through the darkness for any sign of him.

He wasn't there. Or maybe it was just too dark now to see.

My breath came out in little puffs of white as it hit the icy air, but I wasn't cold. Where was he? Had he given up? Cade was huge. There was no way he could have followed me through the maze of metal and bars that held up the bleachers.

I paused, looking around for an opening back to the field.

"You should have kept running."

His voice curled around me in the icy darkness, and I shivered with the way it shot straight to my core and sped up my pulse, my heart pounding in my chest. Spinning around, I tried to see where he was hiding, and ran into a solid brick wall of muscled leather as he dropped down from an opening in the bleachers above. How had he moved so quickly? So quietly?

"Why?" My voice came out in a trembling whimper.

His body caged mine in, pressing me back against one of the pillars and I remembered another pillar, another dark place where he'd cornered me just like this and I'd reveled in it, even as my heart had been breaking.

Would he break it again?

I swallowed past the rising emotion and memories, and watched his jaw clench and unclench as if he was remembering the same thing as I was.

"Because I knew if I caught you, I wouldn't be able to let you go."

Heart thundering in my ears, I gasped as I felt the heat of his body sink into mine through the thick layers of leather and denim between us.

"Who says you have to?"

I felt the brush of his stubble against my cheek as he leaned down, inhaling my scent, his nose grazing along my jaw.

"You've always smelled so good. So sweet." His teeth nipped the tender skin along my jaw and I wrapped my fingers into the soft leather of his jacket, pulling him closer.

"I didn't want to corrupt you with my darkness," he whispered, his lips tracing a path from my jaw to my neck, leaving a trail of heat that contrasted with the cool air. My head tilted back, granting him more access as I let out a breathless response. "That's where you're wrong. I was corrupted long before I ever met you."

He drew back, his eyes narrowing in the dim light. In

the depths of darkness, I could sense his disapproval. "You weren't corrupted," he said. His voice was rough with an emotion I didn't understand. "You were forced to make tough choices at a young age, without fully grasping the consequences."

"But maybe you weren't the innocent angel I always tried to make you into." He grasped my chin, his thumb tracing my bottom lip and instinctively I nipped at it, drawing my teeth across the thick pad of flesh.

"I told you a long time ago, Cade, I was never good. Never perfect. And yeah, I may have been a pawn in my father's games, but I wasn't the only one. You were just as much a victim of our past as I was."

He hissed in response, then growled as his hips pressed into me, his hardness grinding against the sweet spot of flesh hidden behind layers of clothes. Clothes I desperately wished we were out of.

"So where does this leave us, pretty girl?"

I knew what he was asking. Could we leave behind the Cade and Juniper of the past? Could we begin again with something new? It wasn't a question I was prepared to answer. Especially not with Edmund Wild's presence still hanging over us like a dark veil. Obscuring truth from reality and twisting up any hope I had of having a normal life, right along with it. I gave him the only honest answer I could.

"It leaves us right back where we were all those years ago. Are you going to finish what you started, Cade Black? Or are you going to leave a girl high and dry again?" I threw out the taunt, arching a brow as my tongue darted over my lips in nervous anticipation. I wasn't sure if he could even see my facial expressions in the darkness. But the way he chuckled in my ear and the tightening grip on my hip, told me he knew exactly what I meant.

"Fine. We'll play it your way. But Juniper," His voice was a rumble of desire in my ear as he flicked open the button of my jeans and lazily drew down the zipper. "... the next time I tell you to run, don't make it so easy to get caught. It might make me think that you *want* me to chase you."

I hissed as the cold air hit my skin, but it was quickly replaced by his warm hands sliding over my hips, pulling down my jeans and turning me so that I was pressed against the cold, metal pole.

"Maybe I did..." I gasped when I felt his hand glide between my thighs, spreading them just enough to allow him access. I loved the way he felt against my skin, hard and firm, the rough calluses on his fingers adding extra friction to where he touched.

He chuckled and my heart did somersaults. "Is this what you wanted, pretty girl?" His fingers slipped through my wet folds, dipping and curling inside, teasing and tapping until I forgot it was so cold, my breath was coming out in rapid puffs of white. "You wanted me to chase you, catch you, fuck you here in the open?" While we weren't entirely exposed to any prying eyes, the idea sent a fevered rush of desire through me, and I groaned at his filthy words. God save me, but yes, that is exactly what I wanted. Cade the boy had always been so proper with me, such a gentleman. Cade the man was anything but, and I loved every second of it.

"Look how wet that got you. You like the idea of being taken like this, don't you?" His tone wasn't accusatory, but rather awed, as if he was just coming to an understanding that the woman he had bent over in front of him might be able to better understand his own needs and desires because they matched her own.

"If you'd have finished what you started all those years ago, you might have found out." I rocked against his hand, pulling his fingers deeper into me, demanding more from him. He chuckled, and a hand gripped my throat, pulling me back against him even as I felt the thick head of his cock press against my opening.

"Be careful what you wish for, pretty girl. I'm not one of those three-piece suits your father wanted for you. I will fucking wreck you."

"What gave you the impression I wanted someone in a suit? Quit talking and *fucking wreck me.*" I snapped back at him. One way or another, I would get through to Cade that it wasn't his status, or his clothes, or even his family name that could make me want him. It was him. Cade. Just Cade.

He snarled. The growl of it was like a straight shot of adrenaline to my brain, and my pussy. He lined up the head of his thick cock at my entrance and I heard myself whimper with need. And then he was filling me, stretching me fully and completely, taking over as something in him snapped.

Wave after wave of pleasure rocked into me as he pistoned in and out of my pussy. "Oh fuck, Cade…" I felt a pressure on the back of my neck as he pressed forward, bending me over and forcing my back to arch against him.

With another hand, he ripped the zipper of my jacket down, pulling away the thin fabric of my shirt as he exposed my breasts and skin to the cold air. Not that it mattered. I couldn't feel it with my body on fire for the man who was growling in my ear, and the pleasure he created building into a massive inferno inside of me.

Pleasure, pain, the searing cold as my nipples met the metal pole while he drove his hips into me, pushed every dark thought I had out of my mind.

This. This was what I needed.

This was what I needed him to remind me of. What I

needed him to learn now. I wasn't the Juniper from five years ago. I was more. So much more.

His hands on my hips tightened, and he leaned over me, running his tongue along my neck until his teeth found the tender spot and sank into my skin, marking me, claiming me. Owning me just like he'd said he did.

I felt it down to my soul.

I was his Juniper. And he was my Cade.

I came, milking him as the orgasm ripped through me, crying out his name as he swelled and lost control.

As we both lost control.

7

CADE

At her words, something inside of me snapped.

She wanted me? I would give her me. All of me. The good, the bad and the ugly.

I pounded into her tightness with a ferocity I'd never unleashed before. My hips slapping against her ass as she spread her legs and arched her back, like she was made to take me. It felt like the chains on my self-control had finally broken, and I unleashed every dark part of me I had never shared with her—or anyone.

As my teeth grazed against the sensitive spot on her neck, I knew I wanted to mark her, to have her show the world that she was mine. She gasped just as I pulled her flesh between my teeth, sucking, licking, nipping at the tender skin. I wanted to tattoo my name on her damn soul. Just like she'd done to me.

Her body shuddered. Her orgasm ripped through her just as mine peaked, her pussy fluttering around me. The edges of my vision went dark. And I knew something about coming back to this place.

These bleachers.

This memory.

Every dark thing that had happened in the last five years, everything that we'd been through with each other, it was all in the past.

Because all that mattered was this.

Me and her.

My breaths came out in harsh pants, the knife-sharp cold entering my lungs and cooling the feverish drive that had pushed me over the edge.

Jesus Christ, I'd just taken her out in the open like a damn animal.

And she'd asked me to.

Begged me too. And damn it if I didn't want to do it again.

My hands gripped her hips tight as she continued moving against me, lingering in the afterglow of her orgasm. Belatedly, I realized I had her pressed against the freezing steel pole that held up the base of the bleachers, hiding us from view. I pulled her against my chest, gently running my hands down her chilled flesh as I tugged her shirt down and zipped up her jacket, before stepping away to allow us both the space to fix our clothing.

I didn't know what to expect in the frigid silence, but it definitely wasn't the feel of her warm lips against my cheek, or the purr of her voice in my ear. "I'll make it harder to catch me next time if you promise to fuck me just like that when you do."

Dick. Instantly. Hard. Again.

Fuck me, this woman was going to end me. And I'd let her.

I gripped her face and kissed her before I knew what I was doing, her lips parting under mine with a sweet and desperate sigh. The kiss was wild and turbulent. An onslaught of demand and needs that had built up over years and didn't seem to wane, even with the heady glow of sex in the air from the way I'd just fucked her.

And if we didn't take a step back, I was going to do it again.

I pulled back. I had to get control. "You never answered my question."

Her breath escaped her pouty lips in a puff. "I did. I told you I didn't know what I was going to do."

"You're a terrible liar Juniper Wild."

A delicate brow arched in mild amusement, then she turned and climbed her way through the metal bracers toward the school parking lot and her car. I followed behind her, momentarily distracted by the way her jeans hugged the curve of her ass.

When we reached the track, I put a hand on her arm, stopping her. "Juniper…" my voice was a low warning. She might not understand what was happening, but I knew that behind those beautiful eyes, her mind was working a thousand different angles. I needed to know what she was planning so that I could head her off and keep her away from Edmund Wild.

I had to get to him first. I couldn't say why, just that I knew, if Edmund lured Juniper away it would be the end of her. Forever.

She shifted, a shadow passing over her features and for a moment, I thought she might try to deflect again, until finally she sighed in resignation and shook her head.

"Alright. It's nothing I can confirm yet, just a hunch."

I folded my arms and looked down at her with a small frown. "Spit it out."

"When I was in Denver, the sheriff was the one who came to tell me about my dad…" There was a pause as her voice caught. "…I mean, *Edmund.* Shit. I'm never going to get used to that."

"No one said you had to get used to it." I watched as she shoved her hands deep inside the pockets of her jacket, looking off into the distance again, her teeth worrying her full bottom lip.

"Yeah, it's just..." She took a deep breath and released it, as if the thought was a weight in and of itself. "For so long I always wondered what it would be like to have a different father..." Her voice cracked, and something inside of me cracked as well, as I watched her eyes shimmer in the moonlight as she blinked away the tears that threatened to spill. I itched to hold her, but I knew that wasn't what she wanted—or needed, at the moment.

"If your dad had been someone else." I finished for her, giving voice to the pain that she couldn't. Her eyes burned through me as she realized I understood everything she was trying to say without letting it consume her.

"I used to think that about my mom." Half of a laugh bubbled up from somewhere, and I shook my head. "Hell, I thought about it with my dad sometimes too, but honestly, it was more my mom for me. What would my life have been like if she'd stayed? What would my dad have been like?"

She licked her lips and shifted nervously. "Yeah, I guess that would be hard to deal with. At least I had my mom for a little while." Her gaze was full of sympathy and understanding as she gained some control over the emotions that were threatening to break free. "I'm sorry, Cade. I didn't mean to sound uncaring."

"You didn't, pretty girl. I just meant that I get it. And it's ok to wish and wonder about those things. But you can't dwell on it, or you'll spend so much time wishing for what could have been instead of focusing on the *here* and *now*." I rocked back on my heels, ready to put the topic we'd ventured upon to rest. "You think the sheriff has information on Edmund?"

She nodded, breathing warm air into her cupped hands, then we both moved toward the parking lot once more as I shortened my stride to match hers, grabbing one of her hands and tucking it inside the warm pocket of my jacket. The night was near-freezing, and the temperature was dropping faster. I felt like an ass for keeping her outside for so long.

"Like I said, it's just a hunch. But they were close and I found…" Her voice hesitated and she gave me a sidelong glance.

"Go on. What did you find?" We were nearly at her car now, and I made another mental note to get her snow chains ready for the winter roads.

"Well, don't be mad, but I found a file that was filled with a bunch of criminal records, most of it your dad's." The words spilled out of her lips in a rush, and for a brief moment, the old anger and rage threatened to creep in, my hand involuntarily gripping hers tighter. But then I felt her hand squeeze back, her blue eyes searching mine with worry, and I quickly released my grip, rubbing my thumb along the back of her hand in reassurance.

"I'm not surprised. Edmund had tabs on just about everyone in this city. My dad would definitely have been one of them."

"Yes, but how? He wasn't their lawyer. There's no reason he should have had that kind of information on hand." She pulled open her car door and slid inside, as she started the engine and the old VW roared to life with a sputter into the chilly night air. I was honestly impressed that it even managed to do that. I added a full tune-up to the maintenance checklist that I was mentally building, of things the car needed before winter was fully upon us.

"You think he was getting paid to feed him this information?" Once the question left my lips, I realized how much it made sense. There wasn't much in this city that the sheriff didn't know about, and the power that Edmund had over people, had to come from somewhere other than just his money. Information was often a better source of currency than dollar bills.

She looked off into the distance, as if contemplating my words. "I'm not sure." Her voice sounded hollow for the briefest of moments, before her eyes snapped back to mine with a determined look that I recognized immediately. Whatever information the sheriff had, Juniper wasn't going to stop until she had it. "But he's the only other lead I have. I need to talk to him soon."

Not before I do, pretty girl. I smiled and leaned down,

brushing my lips over hers, but before she could give into the kiss, I straightened. "I'll see you later tonight."

"What?" Confusion marred her features as she looked up at me. "Since when do you get to tell me you're coming over?"

"Since now, pretty girl. Text me your alarm code." I slammed her door shut and jogged to where my Bronco was parked and waiting. If she was smart, she'd do what I said, although secretly I hoped she would defy me, just to give me a reason to teach her a lesson again.

She rolled down her window and called out just as I was opening my door. "You aren't the boss of me, Cade Black! And you can't come over. I have plans!"

"Yes, I am, pretty girl. And yes, you do. With me." I winked as I climbed into my car, and she sped away with a grin, shaking her head. I had no intention of going another night away from her. But first, I had a meeting with a certain city sheriff to get to.

8

JUNIPER

I looked down at the message notification as my phone vibrated on the cushion next to me.

Cade: "I haven't gotten that code yet."

Me: …

Me: I don't think so, bossy pants.

Cade: If I have to break in, I will, but I'd rather not. So be a good girl and send it.

Me: I told you, I have plans.

Cade: No, you don't. I know you, Juniper, just like I know that right now you're in your pajamas, eating ice cream, with no plans to go anywhere until at least work this weekend.

I huffed and stared at my phone in annoyance, before picking up the carton of ice-cream I'd carried into the room with me, taking another bite. Damn him. After heading home, showering and wolfing down the delicious stew Bess had waiting for us, I'd changed into my pj's for what was becoming my nightly routine. Combing through Edmund's office for any other clues to his disappearance that I could find. This time, I had a fire roaring though, and most of the dust and old files were cleaned up. The longer I spent here, the less of his presence I felt. As though with each file I went through, and each cobweb I cleared out, a little bit of the shadows that I felt clinging to the walls, receded. I cast a look around the dark walls and decided that it was time to take back this space completely.

Dead or alive, Edmunds presence had to be purged from our lives. And if he was really alive and hadn't contacted us by now, then I could only guess that he had no intention of coming back here anyway, and wouldn't mind the makeover. My phone buzzed again.

Cade: Pretty girl…

Me: I am not sending my alarm code to a crazy stalker.

Cade: Are you saying that I'm a crazy person?

Me: If the shoe fits…

Cade: I look forward to what's coming later.

Me: What's that supposed to mean?

Cade: You'll see.

I rolled my eyes and didn't respond. He was nuts if he thought I was going to send my code to him. I didn't want to tell him why, though. That every night since I'd found the skull painted on my car, there had been footprints that I didn't recognize in my garden and outside my window. That I'd found notes telling me I needed to leave, or watch my back, left in places around my house. Places only I would walk out to and see. That several nights, when I couldn't sleep, I'd go for a walk in the garden only to think I saw a figure on the roof, lurking outside of Dean's room. I'd taken to sleeping with a gun in my nightstand and changing my alarm code often.

I stood up and stretched. It was getting late and once again, my searches had proven unfruitful. All I'd managed to uncover, were some old receipts and the business card to some club in Denver stuck in the back of an old appointment book.

I thought about David Black's arrest record and then glanced down at the photo once more. All of them were there together. At some point in the past, Edmund and David had liked each other enough to be photographed together. So what happened between the two men that made Edmund use me against him? What did David do that made Edmund hate him so much?

Unfortunately, neither man was available to question

it. But maybe there was another possibility. My eyes narrowed as I observed the dark-haired mystery man once more. Something about him drew my eyes to him every time, and it wasn't that he was an unknown figure. There was something oddly familiar about him. As if I'd seen those eyes and that face somewhere before, but I couldn't place where.

I huffed. I didn't even have a name. Just a photograph.

I blinked. A photograph—A photograph with four people standing in front of a fireplace.

There was another photograph with four people standing in front of a fireplace. Four people in masks. With invitations on the front of them, like the invitation tucked away in my bedside table drawer.

And there were names on the back of that photograph.

Excitement coursed through me. I had to find that picture.

But where would mom have put it?

Leaving the office, I walked down the hall to my bedroom. The bedroom that had once been my mother's area of the house. It hadn't been that long since I'd moved in, and much of the room was just as she'd left it. I stood in the center of the room and looked around at the bed draped with a soft down comforter and the pale blue walls. I tried to recall what she had done with the photo when I'd shown it to her, and turned in a slow circle until my eyes landed on something glinting from the adjoining bathroom. A golden-framed photograph of her smiling in the sunshine.

I hurried into the bathroom and snatched up the picture frame, turning it over and sliding the cardboard backing off, my fingers trembling with excitement and nervousness. *Please, please, please.* I whispered over and over in my head as a silent prayer, and felt my stomach flip when I pulled out the faded photograph, its edges tucked in to make it fit inside the tiny frame. Carefully, so carefully so that it didn't rip, I opened the creased edges and was once again staring at the sinister, white-masked figures. Turning the pages over, I nearly screamed with excitement. The names were still there.

E. Wild.

B. DeClare.

D. Black.

N. Diovolo.

I blinked. And blinked again. Diovolo. As in Kage Diavolo.

And B. DeClare. Blaire DeClare. I hadn't recognized the name at the time because I'd been too young to realize that her name hadn't always been Wild. That she'd been something *other* before marrying Edmund. That was why she'd looked so frightened when she saw the photo. She hadn't wanted me to recognize *her.*

But now I knew who the person in the photo was, and I couldn't believe it. Whoever N. Diovolo was, he had a relation to Kage Diovolo. There was no way he hadn't.

And now, I knew who might have the answers to who the mystery man was. Only he was probably the one person I didn't want to ask for help with this, because there was no telling what he'd want in return. Or if this was even information he wanted out in the open. He might kill me before helping me. I swallowed. But there was nothing I could do. I had to know.

I had to uncover the truth, even if it cost me.

And I knew who to ask to get me the answers I needed.

I picked up my phone and hit the dial. It had been weeks since I'd heard my friend's voice, but I knew she'd answer.

Stacy picked up on the first ring. "This had better be good, bitch, because I'm so pissed that you abandoned me to this hellhole." Music was thumping in the background and I knew she was at the Pit working.

I snorted. "Are you saying you'd like me to come back and take over as bar manager?"

"Fuck no. I like the money. But I wouldn't mind if you kicked some of these assholes in the head a time or two. My god they're such babies…one sec." I heard her shout some instructions to some bartenders, and then the music faded as she disappeared into the stockroom to talk to me.

"Okay. What's up, babe? Ready to come back to the real world or are you still going to yippee kai-yay it out there in the wild west?"

I shook my head, grinning, and gently traced the outline of the photo on my bathroom counter. "I'm afraid I'm here for good, doll. But I wouldn't mind making a trip to come see you. *Or,* you could pack up your scrawny ass and come here? Maybe you'd actually like it."

It was her turn to snort and I could almost see her shaking her head, her piercings dancing. "No way. Small city life is not for me. But I'd love to see you. Things have been mostly quiet since you made Jax sing soprano. I could use some fun and shenanigans."

Grabbing the photograph, I left my bedroom and made my way back to the office. It was probably the warmest room in the house when the fire was going. "Jax hasn't been around since I left?" I frowned, thinking about the last night I'd seen him and the rough-looking men he'd been with. Shit. I'd almost forgotten about that in the daze of dealing with Edmund's death and opening up the Emporium.

"No, why, you missing him? Not getting any good dick back there in the wild, wild west? 'Cause let me tell you, there's pleeeenty to go around here.``

I laughed. "Ha! Hardly. I'm just glad he hasn't been around to harass you. And trust me, the dick here is definitely wild. I'm good on that part."

"Ohhh...don't tell me you actually got back with that douche bag that left you high and dry all those years ago." Stacy's voice was teasing, but there was a tinge of concern in her words.

"Well...it's complicated." Complicated was the only way I could describe it. Complicated. Beautiful. Delicate in the way the wildflowers bloomed in the valley in the spring. I pushed down the feeling of giddy excitement. This wasn't the time to unload my rollercoaster of thoughts and emotions when it came to Cade Black.

"Oh suck a butternut, June. You're getting down and dirty with the ex. Please tell me the dick is worth it, at least."

I rolled my eyes and moved to stand in front of the roaring fireplace. The flames leapt, and I couldn't help but think of the flames and smoke that danced in and out of Cade's tattoos on his arms.

"Stacy, I didn't call to talk about my sex life."

She snorted again. "Rude. What else are we going to talk about? You want to hear about how Big Jim got some gross cyst on his ass and has been walking around dropping his pants for anyone that is brave enough to take a look?"

"What? Ew! Stacy, no!" My eyes burned with the visualization. "Listen, I need a favor." I rushed to finish before she could start giving me any details on Big Jim's new party trick, or sending me pictures.

"Oh? What's up?" I could hear her voice perk up with curiosity.

"I need you to get me a meeting with Kage Diovolo."

There was a pause on the other end of the line.

"What the fuck, June. What kind of trouble are you in? Are you crazy?"

"Stacy, please. It's important. He has information I need." I leaned down to grab an iron fireplace poker and jabbed at the crackling logs. Sparks shot up, and the embers burned brighter. Their orange and red glow drew my gaze, and I found myself sitting down in Edmund's leather chair to watch them.

"Look, I don't know what's going on with you there in Wild, but Kage is the one person you should stay far, far away from. He almost never comes to The Pit, you know that. He lets us exist autonomously, so long as there's no trouble and the books balance. But he's been here three or four times in the past couple of months. And he's scary as fuck. Hot. But scary. You need to stay far away from him."

I sighed. "Stacy, please...I need this, and I have no other way of getting in contact with him. Please don't make me call Big Jim."

I could hear her pacing up and down the rows of metal shelving.

"Fine. Fine. I don't want to, but I'll do it. But you should know something, June." She paused, and the fear was palpable on the other end of the phone. "He wasn't just here checking on business. He was asking a lot of questions, a lot of personal questions…" she took a deep breath, "… and he wanted to know about you."

I sat up and gripped the poker tighter. "Me?"

"Yeah, you miss sunshine-out-of-her-ass. You still want me to contact him? Because I think you being in Wild and as far away from anything Kage Diovolo is involved in, is the best thing for you."

She was probably right. Kage asking questions about me wasn't a good sign, and I didn't know what it meant. But there was only one way to find out. And I had questions of my own to ask.

"Just get me a meeting, Stacy. I can take care of myself." I sat back with a frown, my eyes trained on the flickering flames as I thought about what Stacy had just told me. Did Kage know about my mother? Did he know about Edmund?

She sighed. "Okay, June, just please be careful. Okay?"

"Always. Love you, bitch."

"Love you too, bitch." The line went dead.

Kage Diovolo asking questions about me was something I'd never expected or wanted to hear. But it might just work in my favor.

A log popped in the fireplace and I sat back, curling my legs beneath me as the flames leapt higher and my gaze fixed on them.

I didn't even realize when I fell asleep.

9

JUNIPER

I woke to a heavy weight blanketing me.

A thick, muscled leg was thrown over mine and a powerful arm held me snug against a broad chest, while another arm pillowed my head.

I turned my face, and my lips met the warm, hard muscle of his tattooed chest. His shirtless chest that bore tattoos which I'd designed for him all those years ago.

For a brief moment, I questioned how he had gotten in here, or into the house at all, but then I remembered his messages from last night, and decided I didn't want to know.

Wiggling, I tried to get him to loosen his grip, but all he did was shift his hips against me before pulling me closer, and I realized he was completely naked beneath a throw blanket I normally kept on the back of the couch.

The fire had long since died down, and the office was now a freezing box of ice. The only warmth in the room was the giant of a man pressed against me on the couch that we were laying on.

What was it about couches with him? Did he have a thing for sleeping on them?

I huffed and raised my head to check if the office doors were at least closed. The last thing I needed was Dean or Bess to walk by and see Cade in all his tattooed glory, snuggling up to me like a polar bear to an ice-cube. Satisfied that the doors were at least closed and hopefully locked, I rested my head on the pillow of his bicep once more.

I had no idea what time it was, but I knew I needed to get up and find my clothes before anyone else woke up.

But we were alone. And he was naked. The temptation was too much to resist, and it didn't take much for me to wiggle the silk pajama bottoms down my hips.

Cade grunted when I tried to create enough space to remove my top and I froze, thinking I'd woken him up. But then he flipped suddenly onto his back, taking me with him, and I landed squarely on something that was hard, warm and definitely ready to say good morning.

I glared at his peacefully sleeping face and smacked his chest. But he only snorted and continued to breathe in that deep, dreamless sleep sort of way.

Rolling my eyes, I quickly slipped out of my shirt, the cold air kissing my body, before shifting again, only to be met with *Mr. Happy to See Me* rubbing against my very naked center. And damn it if she wasn't equally excited to see him. He let out a grunt as I moved against him, sliding my wetness over the hard length and then back again. If he was going to leave it unattended like this, what was a girl supposed to do? Resist? I grinned and sat up, rocking against him a little harder; the friction sending electric tingles through my body.

One hazel eye peeked open in the dim light. I rocked my hips again, setting a slow and agonizing rhythm, trapping him between our flesh. He gripped my hips with a groan. "Careful, pretty girl." His eyes burned a bright greenish-gold as he gazed up at me beneath hooded lids.

"Careful with what?" I smirked, and did it again, this time rotating my hips and adding more pressure just to hear him hiss with pleasure. "How did you get into my house?"

He tightened his fingers on my flesh, took control of my movements, and slid my slick core against his cock until it pressed against my clit, making me gasp from the pressure and friction.

"I have my ways." He sat up, his mouth latching onto my nipple as he drew it between his teeth, the pain and pleasure sending need coursing through me. "Good thing too. Your teeth were chattering in your sleep."

"So you decided to get naked and cuddle?"

He switched sides, his tongue swirling around the peak as he rocked his hips up into mine, our bodies flush to each other, but the delicious friction was only partly what I wanted. I arched my hips, searching for him, needing to feel him inside of me.

"I decided to delay what I originally had in mind and get you warm instead." He held himself back, not letting me sink down onto his thick length like I wanted. I whined in frustration.

"I need to tell Bess to change the locks."

He smirked as his hand snaked up to grip the back of my head, his fingers winding into my hair, gripping me at the base of my neck and pulling me back just slightly so I could look at him.

"There's not a lock, door or gate that could keep me from getting to you, Juniper Wild. Trust me on that."

"I can't decide if that's romantic or creepy." His thickness was sliding against my opening again, just beyond reach and driving me insane.

"Neither. I am what I am Juniper. I won't apologize for it." Large hands held my hips still, not letting me move and seek the pleasure my body demanded.

My eyes narrowed into slits of frustration. "What you

are is a damn tease. Is this what you had planned? Denying a girl perfectly good morning sex?"

A grin split his lips, and I wanted to gasp at the beauty of his smile. No man should have a smile like that. "No, *that* would make me crazy. And I'm not." He shifted his position and leaned back, lifting my hips until I was suspended just over the broad tip, and could feel it teasing my opening. "Tell me you're mine."

"What?" I blinked, distracted by what I wanted, being so close and yet so far away at the same time.

"Tell me, Juniper. Say it." His smile disappeared and was replaced by a look of such intensity that I shivered. The morning light that came in from the windows cast a dusky-gray shadow across his sharp features, making the scar stand out. Gone was the teasing tone and the husky morning voice. In its place was a dominating demand. His grip on my hips was the same, but he remained poised and tight with tension beneath me.

I stared at him. The words stuck in my throat. Was I his? Yes. Yes. Yes. My heart cried out like a drumbeat in my ears. I was his. I had always been his. Words came back to me. His voice, and the sharp sting of his rejection. *"You could never be mine. Go home Juniper."*

"I was always yours, Cade. Always." His eyes lit up at my whispered admission, then he slammed me down onto his waiting cock, its thick girth filling, stretching and finally easing the ache inside of me.

My spine arched back with pleasure as my hips met his, rocking into him.

"That's it, pretty girl. Ride me."

I leaned forward, taking him deeper as I slid up and down his length, my breasts brushed against his face with the movement. With a guttural snarl, he latched on to one tender nipple, and the spike of pleasure his lips sent through me went straight to my core.

"Yesss…" I hissed, as the pleasure built. "Oh my god, Cade."

He took his time, licking, sucking and teasing the nipple of my breast before turning his attention to the next. All the while letting me take control of the pace, the rhythm. I bounced and rocked.

"Cade, please…" My voice was a whimper of need. I was so close. So close to tipping over the edge. I just needed—

"Come for me, Juniper. Come on my cock. Show me you're mine, pretty girl." He reached between my legs, teasing my swollen clit with his fingers.

Stars burst behind my eyes as his words tipped me over the edge. My pussy fluttered as the orgasm quaked through me. And when I finally opened my eyes, I looked down to see him, heavy-lidded and smirking. He rolled his hips, sending a scattering of pleasure through my body once more as I realized he was still hard and throbbing inside of me.

"My turn." He growled, and then in one swift movement he pulled out, picked me up and bent me over the couch, my legs spread wide. The cold air hit my core, and I hissed as goosebumps raced across my skin.

"Look at you my pretty girl, such a pretty mess for me."

His hands traced my backside, spreading warmth where they went, and I arched my back, exposing more of myself to him.

"A needy, fucking mess." His fingers plunged into my opening and I hissed at the invasion, then moaned when he pulled them out and I felt a sharp slap to my pussy.

"Fuck, you smell so good. Taste so good. Like honey and lavender." His voice rumbled against me as his tongue did a slow, teasing circle around my clit. My voice was a whine of need. "Oh, fuck…"

"I told you it was my turn, pretty girl." His tongue dove deep into my slick core and I sucked in a deep breath to keep from screaming and waking up the entire house. He withdrew it slowly. "Beg me for it, Juniper."

"Cade, please…" I breathed his name like a prayer, and that seemed to satisfy him. He dove back in, his tongue licking and teasing. Driving me once more to the brink of delicious pleasure. I dropped my head, my face buried in the thick cushion of the leather to hide my moans. I couldn't take it. The pressure built and built. Then he was adding his fingers, sliding and curling them over and over against that sweet spot deep inside me. First one finger, then two. "How many more can you take, pretty girl?" I panted, shaking my head. "Cade please...I need..." He added a third finger and I exploded, my body wracked with quakes as my orgasm dripped down around his face, his fingers, his hand.

It took him less than a second to wrap my hair around one hand, yanking my head back as he slammed home inside of me. His hips pistoned in and out in a punishing rhythm. One hand gripped my breast, squeezing, dominating, as he fucked me against the back of the couch.

"My pussy. My Juniper. Mine.' He punctuated each word with a deep thrust, as his orgasm erupted and I felt him spurt hot and thick inside of me. And as he did, it tipped me over into the abyss once more, and I cried out as my release hit, leaving me breathless.

His hips pumped slowly, his breathing harsh as he cradled me against the back of the couch. "Mine." His whispered voice was almost reverent as he pressed his forehead to my back, shuddering inside of me one last time.

I curled my hand around his biceps, covering one of the grinning skulls that glared at me with unseeing sockets, and closed my eyes. "And you're mine." I whispered back.

My eyes traced the line of tattoos, momentarily wondering who had done the beautiful work, until they dipped and stopped at the knuckles, where something darker than black ink marred his skin.

I gasped.

His hands were covered in blood.

10

CADE

I pulled away from her as she held up my hand and turned to look at me.

Fuck.

I'd been so tired, and she'd looked so peaceful sleeping all curled up in the large leather chair, that I'd forgotten about anything other than needing to take care of her. To hold her. To claim her again.

Concern danced in the depth of her eyes.

"Cade, what happened? Are you okay?" She asked, her voice filled with shocked anxiousness.

Concern. Not accusation.

Guilt plagued me. What would she say if I told her the truth?

What would she say if I revealed the darkness inside of

me? That everything her father had ever said about me was true?

I pulled my hand away and shrugged.

"It's nothing. Just an accident with an engine. I didn't stop at my place to shower before I came here."

The lie rolled so easily off my tongue that it made me sick.

Could she tell? Her eyes scanned my face, dipped down the rest of my body, then back up. A smile parted her lips as she leaned in and brushed a kiss against the stubble of my cheek.

"Okay, well—don't expect me to baby you or anything. You're a grown man. There are Band-Aids in the bathroom down the hall."

My stomach clenched, and I reached for my jeans that I'd draped over the back of the couch.

"Noted. You have horrible bedside manners." I kept my voice even, my tone light, and she let out a throaty chuckle that had my balls tightening again.

"Yeah—they kicked me out of nursing school for it."

I paused, one leg in my pants while the other foot hovered over the remaining pant leg to look up at her in surprise. "You wanted to be a nurse?"

She shrugged and pulled on her discarded pajamas. "It was more of a *do anything to get away from slinging drinks while dodging ass grabs and make something of myself* type of decision. I saw an ad for some assistant nursing classes and took a chance on it. But apparently, they frown upon telling patients to *suck it up* when you're trying to draw their blood."

Buttoning my jeans, I scrutinized the rest of my clothes for any other evidence of last night's activities.

I knew I'd changed, and the plastic bag full of bloodied clothes that were still in the back of my Bronco would have to be incinerated. But the cuts on my hands had opened back up. Normally, I was very meticulous about these things. Coming to her home in the middle of the night with blood dripping down my hands and rage clouding my vision, perhaps wasn't the smartest decision.

But after what I'd seen, what I learned, the only thing I'd had on my mind was getting to Juniper. I needed to see her, feel her, touch her and know that she was safe. That she was okay.

The sheriff had been one sick fuck.

But I couldn't tell her that. I couldn't inform her about what I had discovered and the images that had been burned into my brain forever.

The good sheriff hadn't been home when I'd broken into his house, and it was apparent that he hadn't been expecting company either, because it was all too easy to do a quick once-over of the house and find the poorly hidden box of polaroids in his tiny study.

Polaroids filled with blonde hair and glacier, lake-blue eyes. The sheriff had thought himself untouchable to leave such filth like this so out in the open.

My hands had shaken violently as I'd made a call to a friend who had skills that I'd never be able to possess, and in a matter of minutes, had access to the sheriff's firewall protected private server.

My only question to her had been, "Is he on the list?"

Her response had chilled me to the bone. "He is now. If you don't handle it, Black, I will."

I didn't ask any more questions or even want to know. The photos in the box were enough to sign his death warrant.

He'd found me waiting for him in the darkened study, twirling one photo between my fingers. One of the few I could find where clothes were involved.

He didn't seem as surprised as I'd hoped he'd be. Or scared.

The only words he said before I launched myself at him were, "So, you've finally come."

I blacked-out after the first punch.

And didn't come-to until I was staring down at a mangled mass of flesh and brain matter.

I'd left the way I'd come in, slipping through an open window and into the chilly night air like a shadow.

Another phone, different from my regular cell, and another phone call, one for emergencies such as this. A rough voice spoke on the other end of the phone, this one male and curt.

"Coordinates?"

I rattled off the address.

"Shit, that's the sheriff's—"

I cut him off. "I know where the fuck it is. Just get it cleaned up, Ric."

"Are you back, Black? Cause if you are, you can get fucked if you think I'm going to be throwing you a welcoming party."

"I'm not back, dickhead." I slipped between the shadows of tall trees and brick buildings, my eyes scanning for any witnesses or pesky doorbell cameras. This was so completely off from the way I usually took out my targets, that I was more pissed at myself for losing control like that.

Control kept everything from getting out of hand.

Control kept things clean and efficient.

Control kept the black rage from overtaking me.

Control kept me from going back to prison.

"Then why are you calling me? This number is for

Diablo business only." Ric growled into the line. "I'm not sticking my neck out for you."

"Trust me Ric, this *is* Diablo business. And if Kage finds out you left me out to hang, it will be more than your neck on the line. Get a fucking clean-up crew out here, now." I'd made it to my Bronco, the matte black paint job doing a good job of hiding it among the shadows of the dark alley where I'd parked it.

I didn't wait to hear if he would obey. The threat of the President breathing down his neck would be enough. And if he fucked up the job, it would likely be Kage, himself that would remove Ric's ugly mug from his useless neck, and probably several other body parts as well.

Then I'd smashed the burner phone under my foot and kicked the pieces toward a sewer gutter before climbing into the cab and taking off toward Juniper's place.

Breaking in had been easy. Her flimsy security system was something I could bypass in my sleep. I'd searched her house one room after the other, until I finally found her curled up in the oversized leather chair, her blonde hair fanned out over the arm like a waterfall, those pouty lips I'd dreamt about for years turned down in a frown, as she tried to snuggle into the chair for warmth. The fire in the fireplace had long since burned out, and the room was freezing.

I'd gathered her in my arms and wrapped my body

around hers, covering us with a blanket that had been draped over the back of the couch. Somewhere in the middle of the night, the combined heat of our bodies had me stripping out of my clothes. Or maybe I was still subconsciously trying to get as close to her as possible.

I finished pulling on the long-sleeved thermal, the only other shirt I'd had in my Bronco, and turned to see her with her ear pressed against the thick, double doors of the office. I might have smiled at how adorable she looked with her hair pulled up high in a messy bun and her soft, striped pajamas accentuating her curves, but then I caught sight of my hands again.

I'd fucked her with these bleeding and bruised hands. Hands that had ripped apart a man who didn't deserve to breathe the same air as her. I'd fuck her in a pool of my blood if it meant she was safe. If it meant she was protected. If it meant I could keep her away from the darkness that was my world.

Did Juniper know? Did she remember? The sheriff had been a sick bastard, but it took an even more deranged and vile piece of shit than him to exploit a child like that. And I knew of only one disgusting person who fit the mold. The dark beast that lurked just under my skin threatened to consume me again, and I had to take a few deep breaths to clear my head. *He would pay. The fucking bastard would pay.*

Juniper pulled open one door and tossed a smile over her shoulder at me. "No one's up yet. I'll make some coffee, and then you can tell me how and why you snuck into my house last night."

"The *how* you don't get to know." I followed her into the dimly lit hall. The light from the morning sun was just beginning to filter through the windows that framed either side of the large entry door, casting a soft glow over the threadbare carpet. Something about the faded carpet triggered a thought. I'd gathered from other things that Juniper and Dean had both said, that their father's death hadn't left them in the best of ways financially. But Edmund Wild had been the wealthiest businessman in the county. So what happened? "But as for the reason..." I grabbed her elbow, stopping her mid-stride and pulling her against my chest before leaning down to capture her mouth in a slow kiss. "You already said you're mine, pretty girl. And I plan to wake you up like that as much and as often as I can. Any complaints?"

Her blue eyes blinked up at me with a haze of desire and amusement, but she didn't pull away. "Hmm... maybe not about the wake-up. But we need to talk about your lack of personal boundaries." She grinned and gave me a pat on the chest. "Go clean up, big boy. I'll see if I can find us something to eat." Then she headed toward the kitchen while I stepped into the small powder room to clean up.

My phone buzzed in my pocket just as I finished drying my hands, and I cursed when I saw the name as well as the number of missed calls. But Kage would have to wait. No doubt he'd already deduced what I'd discovered, and was more pissed about the fact that I'd handled the sheriff before he could. For now though, I had to find out what Juniper had been up to the past several days, and why she'd fallen asleep holding a picture of Kage's dad.

11

JUNIPER

With his kiss and a smile still lingering on my lips, I made my way into the kitchen and pulled out the coffee beans and grinder. I wasn't a semi-professional chef like Cade was, apparently, but I could at least make coffee. Or something that passed for coffee. While the smell of freshly brewed bean juice filled the kitchen, I rummaged around the pantry for something semi-edible. A familiar tupperware container caught my eye, and I nearly squealed with glee. Bess's famous lemon and blueberry scones made my stomach rumble with hunger. How they'd escaped Dean's bottomless pit of a stomach, I didn't know, but I sent up a prayer of thanks as I pulled out the dish and set it on the kitchen island.

I fingered the polaroid photos that I'd picked up off the floor, tucking them into the pocket of my pajamas as I was getting dressed. Had Cade noticed them? I wondered if Cade would be as shocked as I had been to see that it seemed like our parents had at least been friendly with each other at one point. Something we were both raised to believe would only have happened if hell froze over. My gaze traced over my mother's face, her smiling eyes and the softness in them as she gazed at the mystery man. I'd never seen her look like that when she was alive. It was too early to text Stacy and see if she'd made any progress with Kage Diovolo. More than likely, she'd still be sleeping off her shift at The Pit, or a hangover. Probably both knowing Stacy.

Cade had told me that my brother wanted to meet with me. But then, I hadn't heard a peep from either of them for weeks until Cade had shown up at Dean's school. Now he was back in my house and I had more questions than answers. I decided then that he wasn't leaving until I had a few of them answered. I eyed the scones, debating on whether or not I should hide a few for later. Who knew how hungry Cade would be?

The man himself appeared in the doorway, leaning casually against it with his arms crossed over his chest. The fabric of his thermal shirt pulled taut, highlighting the thick curve of his muscled shoulders and biceps. *Holy shit.* I tore my gaze away, determined to not get distracted or drool in front of him, but not before I caught the smirk that curled at the corner of his lips, and the teasing tone of his voice. "Did you make that for me, pretty girl?" He nodded his chin to the counter where I'd placed the plate of scones and two steaming mugs of coffee.

I picked up one scone and glared at him. "Did I make them? No. I'm a walking kitchen disaster. Am I offering them to you? Also no. These things are like gold around here." I waved the scone in front of his nose as he moved to stand closer to me. "But answer some questions and I'll consider sharing with you."

A brow arched in amusement as he leaned to snap his teeth playfully at my hand. "If you're trying to bribe me, I know something else that would get me talking a lot faster than scones." The heat in his gaze had me sucking in a breath. *Focus Juniper, focus! You want answers, not orgasms.*

"Answers over orgasms? Interesting..." Cade grinned, and before I could close my mouth which hung open in shock, he'd reached around me and snagged a scone for himself, popping the entire thing in his mouth. Had I really just said that?

"What—" I glared at him and pulled the plate away. "No scones for you! I need answers."

He cocked his head, his gaze still heated as he gave me a slow once over, his gaze heating. "I don't know, pretty girl, I think I prefer orgasms."

I rolled my eyes in exasperation. "Cade, be serious."

Something in my tone must have made him realize I was nervous, the anxiousness bleeding through. Was I really going to ask him? Was I really going to share the information I'd found with him? *Yes.* My heart sped up. No more secrets. No more lies. Cade had a right to know.

He eyed me expectantly, those hazel eyes searching mine, and I cleared my throat. "I found something, and I think you should see it. It's about your dad."

"You already told me about the file." A small frown creased his forehead, crinkling the scar that I couldn't help but think was sexy as hell.

"This isn't about the file. Although, maybe it's related. I'm just not sure how, yet." I slid the photo of the four smiling people across the counter to him. "I think our parents used to be friends. I don't think our families were always the enemies they made us out to be."

Cade's frown deepened as he picked up the photo and studied it. If it shocked him or he had any knowledge of who was in the photograph, he gave nothing away. His features remained blank except for the frown. "This is just a picture, Juniper. It doesn't really tell us anything."

"Well then, maybe this picture does." I pulled the second photo out, the one with the people in masks, and slid it toward him. "Look at the names on the back."

His scar glinted in the morning light as he looked at

the photo and then at me. "This is the masked photo you told me about?"

I nodded, fingers tightening on my coffee mug in anticipation. Would he know?

He flipped the photo over and genuine surprise crossed his handsome face. Hazel-green eyes flicked up at me over the photo. "You think our parents were involved in this..." he paused, searching for the word, "...group?"

"They were involved in something." I shrugged and picked up another scone, taking a bite and letting the familiar burst of flavors settle my nerves. "But what, I can't say. And if our families were friends at one point, what happened to make them hate each other so much?"

I took a sip of my coffee and observed him. He'd made no mention of the other man in the photo. Almost purposefully. A gnawing suspicion grew. "Who is he?"

Cade's mouth thinned into a grim line but he didn't answer me.

I set my mug down.

"You know who he is."

"Juniper..." His voice was a low growl of warning.

"No." I blinked as realization dawned. "You *knew* who he was even before I showed you that picture."

"Juniper, I didn't know about the picture or anything that you've shown me so far." He was being purposely evasive, and it was pissing me off.

"What aren't you telling me, Cade?" I pushed away from the counter and angrily poured the rest of my coffee down the sink. I didn't have the stomach for it anymore. "Since I've come back, you've done nothing but harp on my ass for lying to you all those years ago, and yet, here you are withholding information from me."

"That's not the same as ly—," I whirled around, my hands shaking as I gripped the edge of the counter and cut him off.

"Oh fuck you and semantics. Yes it is. You can throw sprinkles on shit but at the end of the day, it's still shit. It still stinks." I grabbed the photos and held them up. "And this smells like a massive pile of sprinkle-covered shit." I was seething now, the kitchen island suddenly becoming a buffer between us. A no-mans land of space that connected and divided us at the same time. Was this how it was always going to be between us now? Bridges mended only to break apart at the first strong gust of wind?

Cade only gave me that blank stare that said he wasn't going to reveal anything. "I'm telling you the truth. Call it shit, call it whatever you want. This is the truth. I know nothing about these photos. I know nothing about why our parents seem to be friends here."

"But you know something about the man in that photo."

His jaw flexed, the muscle ticking in agitation. "I know something. That's all I can say."

"Then you can leave." I was done with this bullshit. I'd opened up my cards and laid them all out on the table for him to see. I'd held nothing back. But it looked like Cade was still not willing to be as open with me.

"Juniper," I cursed the way my name on his lips sent tingles through me, even when I was raging, seething, at him. "I was going to say that's all I can say because I'm not the person you need to be talking to." His voice was flat, as if he'd shoved all emotion behind a steel wall.

"Oh, you mean like this mysterious brother I've never met? And tell me, exactly *when* am I going to be allowed to ask him questions? You protect him like he's the fucking President or something." Was I a little bit pissed that the brother I'd never met still hadn't come forward to introduce himself? Maybe. I heard a phone vibrate on the countertop.

"Now, actually." Cade was looking at his phone with a frown creasing his handsome face.

"What?" Suddenly my mouth was dry. He couldn't be serious. I hadn't heard from Stacy yet. I needed my meeting with Kage before I met the man who was supposedly my brother. I needed to be armed with information, and I was most definitely not.

Cade's jaw tightened as he looked up. He didn't like

this either. "Your brother is waiting for us. He's at my shop now." He stood up and stepped away from the counter. "Get dressed, Juniper. You're about to get the answers to all of your questions. I just hope you're ready for them."

My world tilted as I watched him storm off to the front of the house, his phone pressed to his ear, but I was too lost in my own thoughts to hear what he said. I was going to meet my brother. I should be excited, happy.

Why did it feel like I was going to meet my fate?

12

JUNIPER

ade's Bronco was very much a reflection of the man himself. Completely blacked-out with plush leather seats, tinted windows, and not a single spec of dust or dirt anywhere to be seen. For a man that lived and grew up in the mountains of Colorado, this was almost unheard of. I almost wanted to apologize for the wet print my boots had left on the rugged floor mats, then I decided I was still too angry at him to apologize for anything.

A light dusting of snow had greeted us when I'd finally pulled myself together enough to come downstairs. I'd stalled as long as I could, trying to get Stacy to answer my phone calls and text messages, but she never responded. I could only assume she'd see the half dozen calls and messages, and would call me back as soon as she was awake. Cade had refused to go on without me. Just like he'd also refused to let me drive myself into the city, claiming that my car was a rolling death trap on icy roads. He wasn't wrong. I just hadn't had the time or the money to put the right tires on it, but that didn't mean that I wanted to ride with him.

He backed me up against the side of his SUV and told me I could either be pissed at him and get in the damn SUV, or go back upstairs, get fucked until I couldn't see straight, and then get in the damn truck. My choice, but either way I was riding with him. The heat in his eyes, the press of his hard body against mine, and the way my body wanted to immediately say yes to the hard, angry fucking he promised, told me he meant what he said. He must have noticed my hesitation, or saw the flush in my cheeks because all he did was smirk and open the door for me. "That's what I thought. Get in, pretty girl. You can tell me how angry you are with me later with my cock in your mouth."

"Get fucked, Cade Black." I snarled back at him, even as I buckled up my seatbelt and sank into the warm leather.

"I plan to, Juniper Wild." He shot back, slamming my door shut with enough force that the vehicle shook. Cade was on edge. More than I'd ever seen him before. Something about this meeting was making him nervous, and that made the pit of anxiousness in my stomach grow. I watched the mountain views slide past as I cast a look out of my peripheral to the man next to me. His entire body was rigid and emanated an air of violent energy. Who was he?

The thought startled me. Who was Cade Black? I'd only known him as the boy I fell in love with. The boy I wasn't supposed to fall in love with. Then when I came back, he'd been a whole different man. A business owner. I glanced at the luxurious interior. A successful one, it seemed. The social media images I'd seen of him came to mind. A bit of a playboy, too. Not that I could blame the ladies. Cade was sexy as fuck, and the muscles and tattoos only enhanced that bad boy allure. But that had only told me about the man he'd been since he'd come back to Wild.

Who had he been *before?*

My gaze fell on the scar that sliced through his face and stopped just above his cupid's bow lips. I realized that I'd rushed so fast into wanting the forgiveness of the boy who had haunted my dreams for the last five years, I'd never once stopped to consider who the man might be. Could someone really change that much?

"Where did you learn to cook?" I blurted out, before I could stop myself. I'd been determined to ignore him the entire ride into the city since he'd already said he wouldn't answer any of my questions about my brother, but now I found a new curiosity dominating my thoughts.

My question startled him out of whatever dark train of thought he had been focused on, and he flicked his hazel-green eyes to find mine. For a moment, I thought he wasn't going to answer me, but then his growly voice finally broke the silence. "In prison."

"Oh." The unexpected answer made my heart ache, causing me to shrink back into silence, fearing the consequences of probing further. But then he cleared his throat and continued on.

"They offered classes to us. A lot of the guys took mechanic classes or carpentry, hoping to get jobs when they got out." He shrugged. "But I already knew my way around an engine, so I took cooking classes and business classes. I have a degree in business management." That little breadcrumb of information surprised me, and I turned to study him more.

"You got your degree while in prison?"

He nodded. "Yeah. Not much else to do when you're in a nine by fifteen cell all day, every day, except read and study." The casual way he said it made my heart ache. Edmund had done this to him. Had done this to *us*. My desire to find him and make him pay only grew stronger. I had to find answers, and I had to find them now.

"What made you choose business?" I was genuinely curious now, trying to piece together the bits of Cade's life that were a complete blank for me over the past five years.

We'd both journeyed down such different paths, and yet both of them had led us right back here to Wild. Why?

His fingers gripped the steering wheel tighter, as if on instinct or memory, but then he relaxed. "Honestly, your dad." There wasn't any malice in it or anger in his voice, just pure honesty.

"What? My dad—Edmund? But why?" I couldn't fathom how Cade would be influenced in any positive way by the man who'd despised him so much.

"I never wanted to be in a position where I could lose everything like my dad did." He didn't look at me as he spoke, but then again, his eyes needed to focus on the winding turns down the mountainside. "Edmund was a lawyer and a businessman. He outmaneuvered my dad because he understood how the system worked. So I learned how it worked, too."

"Oh..." My voice trailed off as I realized how much the choices of our parents and our past had influenced us. Cade had gone to prison and come out of it better equipped to fight back. I'd run away and come back better equipped to do—what? What had I done but waste the years partying, working dead-end jobs and above all being a shitty sister? Gray snow clouds filled the sky, reflecting the mood my thoughts had taken. We were getting close to Cade's shop now.

"As for the cooking classes." It was my turn to have my

dark thoughts interrupted. He cast me that lazy, playboy grin that I'd seen captured so many times over social media. "Well, let's just say I like to eat."

I rolled my eyes as we came to a stop outside of the shop entrance. It looked like there was no one there, and yet I was sure that the shop hours said it was open. I turned to Cade with a frown. "There's no one here."

"He's here." He stated flatly. Cade's face was once more schooled into an emotionless mask. "I closed the shop for the day."

"Cade, who the fuck is my brother? You're treating this like I'm about to meet royalty or something." A nervous laugh bubbled up as Cade slid out of his seat and came around to open my door.

"It's actually the other way around, Juniper." A voice came from behind Cade and something stirred in my memory. I knew that voice. My gut clenched.

"I promise I'm no king. I'm only a man." Cade stepped out of the way and a wide grin greeted me, white teeth glinting against tawny skin, with coal-black eyes filled with what could only be described as triumphant delight. Kage Diovolo came toward me, his hand extended in greeting, and the very air seemed to be sucked out of my lungs.

"I have been looking for you for a long time, little sister."

13

JUNIPER

"No. Fucking. Way."

I stood rooted to the asphalt of the shop's parking lot and stared at the man who stood in front of me. Kage Diovolo was my *brother?* A thousand thoughts went through my mind, a thousand scenarios, a thousand denials. But the truth had stared me in the face in the form of a discarded polaroid and an obscure name scratched out and hidden decades ago. A secret affair. A story only half-told. And now, I was staring at the other side of the page.

My brother. The Diablo himself. I couldn't believe it. And yet, I could. Pieces of the puzzle clicked into place.

Kage's hand dropped when he realized I wasn't going to make a move to shake it, his head tilting in that predatory way that left a person wanting to find the quickest route to escape his notice, and never find yourself caught in his attention again. I felt Cade's warm hand slip into mine, subtly pulling me closer to his side. I realized Cade hadn't quite moved out of the way, so that his large frame partially blocked mine. He was being protective. Why did I need protection from my own brother? A glance back at Kage told me he'd noticed, and the glare he cast at Cade said he wasn't happy about it, but he didn't comment. Instead, he turned and swept his arm toward the shop. "Cade has graciously let us use his shop for this first meeting. Hopefully, once we get to know each other better, there won't be any need for a buffer between us. But I thought neutral ground and some privacy might be better for our first talk." He smiled at me and for the first time ever, I saw some genuineness in it. And was that hope? Was Kage actually nervous about this? About meeting me? The thought almost shocked me as much as the knowledge that he was my brother. My mother had slept with Kage's father. It was going to take *a lot* for me to get past that idea.

I nodded and Kage turned around, leading us inside straight to Cade's office like he owned the place.

Sitting down onto the couch, Cade slid in next to me, his body pressing next to mine despite the room, and Kage pulled the desk chair around to the front to face us.

If he noticed how close Cade was sitting next to me, never letting go of the bodyguard vibe, he didn't comment.

"I'm sure you have questions—" He started, and I immediately interrupted him.

"Did you hurt Stacy?"

Black eyes blinked at me, and he cocked his head in curiosity. "I'm sorry, who?"

"Stacy, my best friend. The new bar manager at the Pit." I leaned forward, not caring if he was The Diablo, my brother or anyone else. Stacy still had not returned any of my messages or phone calls, and if Kage was so insistent on privacy, I could only imagine what he would do if he suspected someone knew about our relationship.

"Ahh yes, Stacy." He gave me a smile that didn't quite reach his eyes. "Lots of piercings, nervous talker. Good bartender though." He shook his head. "No clue why you'd think I'd waste time hurting someone who is in my employ." The drip of sarcasm was heavy in his voice. "But I have not seen or heard from your friend since my last visit to the Pit a few weeks ago."

"Oh..." Worry gnawed in my gut. Why hadn't she called me back yet? "Are you sure? I asked her to set up a meeting and—"

Understanding dawned in his eyes. "And now I'm here, but you haven't heard from your friend." His smile turned more reassuring. "I haven't spoken to her but, if it will make you feel better I'll have someone check with my office." He pulled out his phone and sent off a quick text. "Now, as I was saying, I'm sure you have questions?" his voice trailed off, and I instinctively glanced up at Cade, who was watching me, but remained silent. Only squeezing the hand he'd never let go of, as if to reassure me and say it was safe.

I took a deep breath.

"You said you've been looking for me for a long time. How did you know about me, but I never knew about you?" The nervousness in my stomach eased. Finally, I was getting answers.

He cleared his throat and sat back. "That's more complicated to answer than you'd think."

"Try." My voice was flat, dry. I was not in the mood for word games or deflections. Cade squeezed my hand once more, his thumb gently grazing my knuckles in comfort as I cleared my throat, amending my tone. "Please."

Kage sat back and rested one leg across his knee, observing me with a small smile dancing around his lips. The gold skull earring he never took off, danced with every movement. "You may look like your mother, but you definitely take after our side of the family. Our grandfather would have liked you, I think."

Cade snorted at that and both of us looked at him, Kage with a glare and me with mild curiosity, but he didn't say anything else. I turned back to Kage. "But not our father?"

"Oh, Niko would have adored you. If he had lived long enough to know you." A flicker of pain lanced through my heart and I realized I'd been holding out a hope that my real father was still alive. "But Papa would have loved your spirit. He was fond of spirited women." There was a flash of something in his dark eyes that made me question whether or not that was a compliment to the senior Diovolo.

"Is he alive? Our grandfather?" I'd never met my mother's family. Both her parents had died before I was born. And Edmund had never mentioned his parents. In fact, I hardly remember ever asking about them. It was as if they had never existed.

"No," Kage scoffed, his eyes appearing flat and cold. A whisper of a chill shuddered down my arms, as if Death himself had been drawn into our conversation and had reached out to just barely brush against my skin. "He would have liked your spirit, Juniper, but trust me when I say, only to relish breaking it."

"You call him Papa, and our father, Niko. Why?" I was missing something.

Kage nodded. "Yes, old habits die hard, I suppose. When our father was killed, our grandfather adopted me. He had me call him Papa, and I was not allowed to speak about my real father ever again. I could only refer to him by his given name, if that."

That seemed so harsh, I didn't understand. "But why? Why would he do that to you? To his son?"

"Because my father wanted nothing to do with the Diovolo family business. He rejected it, and as a result, our grandfather disowned him. It was as if he'd never existed in our family. No one was allowed to speak of him. He was shunned completely." Kage's face darkened with the memory. "When our grandfather found out he'd been murdered, he immediately retrieved me and told me I was now his son."

"That seems harsh." There was more that Kage was obviously not telling me, but I didn't want to press.

"It was. But that is our life." His face hardened, his gaze never leaving mine. "That is why I'm telling you this. You have a chance right now, Juniper to walk away. You've met me. You know who I am. You can let this knowledge rest and never peel back the curtain of your past. Go back to your life, to your Emporium, to your shop, and your friends and your brother. I will never darken your door again. The people sending notes? I will deal with it. Edmund? He will be found and he will pay for his crimes. You and your brother will be safe." Dread began to fill me as he leaned forward. "You can have the life you want, free from all of this." A hand waved in the air. "But you will never have answers. You will never know who you truly are. That's the deal. That is my gift as your brother, to my long-lost little sister."

I paused, studying him, taking in every inch of him. The air of death and danger clung to my brother like it was a second skin. The brush of death I'd felt hadn't been my imagination. He was sitting in front of me and telling me I was his blood. I only had one question before I made my decision.

"How did our grandfather die?"

Kage didn't smile. Didn't even blink. Just stared at me in that predatory way that made me feel like I was under a microscope, and he was dissecting every single part of me down to the depths of my soul.

"I killed him." He stated simply.

14

KAGE

I waited, willing my body to stay still. To not show all my cards. My sister was even more beautiful than I'd remembered from her interview all those years ago when she'd stood in my club and asked me to give her a job, no questions asked. The man I was five years ago might have blown this opportunity and forced her to my side out of ego and spite.

But not now. Now I am a patient man. I'd waited this long, I could wait longer still, for compliance. And she would comply. The carrot I'd dangled in front of her was too much to resist. I could already see the gleam in her eye as she considered my words. The hunger for truth and knowledge, and the inner-war she waged within herself as she thought about her little brother and what this meant for him.

I knew what her answer would be before she even tipped her chin up, so defiant, so very much like our father, that it almost made me smile. She would come to my side. She might look like Blaire DeClare returned from the dead, but she was a Diovolo through and through. Now that I was sitting across from her like this, I felt like a complete idiot for not seeing it sooner. I was looking for someone who looked like me, assuming that the genes that dominated my family line would also be dominant in her. But apparently the universe had a sense of humor, and the very creature destined to bring about the destruction of her entire family, would no doubt be the spitting image of the woman who had been the ruin of mine.

Juniper shifted, her face so openly readable it was almost painful. She would have to learn to mask those emotions better if she was going to survive what was coming. They would eat her alive, otherwise.

"I'm not running." Her silky voice was quiet, but firm. I could see why Cade had fallen for her. A complication that would force me to tread carefully. Cade was notoriously protective of those he cared about, to include myself. Something I'd exploited time and time again. Would he turn on me against his better judgment if he thought I was a threat to Juniper? My eyes slid to the man in question, as I observed the way he pressed against her.

His thigh nearly dwarfed hers, crowding her space and yet, she didn't draw away from it, instead keeping hers pressed firmly against him. Almost as if she was lending some of her strength to him.

To be honest, I still hadn't decided if I was a threat to my new found sister or not. Diovolo's were notoriously loyal and ruthless at the same time. My grandfather's treatment of my father, for example. The night he was murdered, my grandfather had suddenly appeared at my father's penthouse, looked down at me and said, "Your father was dead to me. Outcast. But now he is murdered. My only son, my Niko. You will come with me, boy, and you will avenge his death one day. And pray that I never cast you out like I did him."

From that moment on, I knew only two things. My father was gone, and I would be my grandfather's revenge. I wasn't allowed to call him grandfather. He was my Papa now. As if by adopting me, he had erased my father from ever existing. Nikolai Diovolo was a name never uttered, except to fuel the desire to avenge his death. I was brought up solely by the old man and raised to take over as the head of the family, once I'd wrestled control from his cold, dead hands.

Yes. My father was murdered. And in turn, I'd killed the man who I held truly responsible for his death. At the end of the day, it was my grandfather who'd driven my father away. And no amount of beatings could erase that memory from my mind.

But there were others who were responsible as well. The person who'd truly killed him that fateful night, for one. And Blaire DeClare, the woman he'd risked everything for, who'd drawn him away from his family, his son, to be there with her.

I didn't blame Juniper at all. She was innocent in it. But that didn't mean that I wouldn't use her as a means to an end. Sister or not.

"No one said anything about running, Juniper. This is an offer I won't extend again. Rip up that invitation and go back to your old life. Live in peace and pretend this never happened." My fingers tapped on my knee, drumming a rhythm only I knew and could hear. Tap-tap, tap-tap. Slow your heartbeat, control your breathing, give nothing away.

She leaned forward, withdrawing her hand from Cade's and the sweet thrill of victory rushed through me. I had her. But it was the viciousness in her voice that made my perspective of her shift, just slightly. "You clearly didn't hear me, brother. I said, I'm not running. And that's exactly what you're asking me to do. You think Edmund Wild cares if I decide I'm done playing his game? He doesn't. He never did. And I don't know what the big, bad Kage Diovolo is capable of..." Her hand waved dismissively in the air and I had to hold back a laugh. Oh, little sister had a bark. But did she bite? "... but I'm almost certain that if you could have found Edmund by now, you would have. So, thank you, but I don't think I trust your promise of protection or that you'll be out of my life forever if I take your offer. I think you very much want to be involved in my life whether I want it or not. Isn't that what you said? 'I've been looking for you for a long time, little sister.'" She mockingly quoted my earlier words. Then she sat back giving me a pointed stare, and I had to suck in a breath for how much she looked like our father at that moment. "Now, *big brother,* are you going to quit with the cryptic bullshit and tell me what I want to know? Or are we done here?"

I couldn't recall the last time I'd felt so exposed in this way. What did she know? What had she learned in the time since she'd discovered I existed? I cast a glance at Cade, but all he did was give me a pointed look that said, *"You have no clue what you've gotten yourself into, bro. Good luck."*

Clearing my throat, I sat back. "Well, okay then. I'm glad to see you don't run from a fight." She didn't blink at my compliment, just continued to stare at me in the same way that I was sure she'd stared down unruly bikers at The Pit. Now I understood why most of my crew had taken to frequenting the bar over the years. This spitfire of a woman, my long, lost little sister had kept them all in line and coming back for more. I was almost glad I hadn't realized who she was then, because I was sure I'd have murdered over half of my club over her. "So, what is your first question?"

"No. I won't run from a fight ever again." There was something there in her voice that I would have to explore later. She took a deep breath, exhaling it slowly as if shaking off the weight of her thoughts, re-centering herself and then asked the question I'd been waiting to answer.

"Who murdered our father?"

"Haven't you figured it out yet, little sis?" My lips curved into a wicked smile as my words dripped with venom. "The same man who murdered your mother. Edmund Wild."

I watched the color drain from her face.

And suddenly I didn't feel as victorious as I had moments earlier.

15

JUNIPER

He was lying. He had to be. My mother died from an illness. She'd been bedridden and sick.

Memories of the cold way Edmund had treated her as she became increasingly more ill flooded back. I'd mistaken his distance for grief. But was it something else?

The base of my skull began to tighten, the first twinges of a headache. I ignored it and focused on the man in front of me. "My mother was sick. How could Edmund have killed her?"

"What if I told you that the money your father had was never his?" Those inky-black eyes stared into mine and I examined his face, searching for myself in his features. His dark brows arched in perfect points over his eyes. His nose was strong, slightly hooked, as if he'd taken a blow to it and never quite got it set right. Or it had just been set too late. His cheekbones were sharp and high, the kind of cheekbones that I knew girls would scream over. My brother was handsome in the way a prowling black panther was dangerous. Beautiful to look at, lethal to get close to. Could I trust him, though?

"You're saying he was broke?" Kage's nod of confirmation made me shift uncomfortably.

"What was your father's occupation?" His lips curved in a practiced, polite smile, but behind it I knew he was all sharp teeth and viciousness.

"He was a lawyer and a businessman, but you knew that. Quit fucking patronizing me Kage. Are you saying Edmund purposely made my mother sick to kill her and take the money? But how? He had money of his own." Disgust churned in my belly. My temples throbbed.

"Did he? Just because he said he was a businessman doesn't mean he was a good one." His head tilted, and he studied me. "People make enemies, Juniper. The man who raised you made a lot of enemies."

"As for *how* he murdered your mother, without exhuming the body and running tests, we can only guess." He shrugged and dismissed my tone as if it was irrelevant.,"But it wasn't just money that Edmund was after.

There was something far more precious and valuable that he wanted control over."

I frowned, trying to think of what Edmund might want that he didn't already have. Even the idea of him killing my mom for money seemed far-fetched. But then I remembered the rotting stairs and the empty bank accounts, and suddenly the idea didn't seem so far out of left field after all.

When I didn't answer, Kage spoke up again. "You, Juniper. He wanted control of *you*." My heart sped up. The looks, the tasks, the long lectures about my role in the family. My place as a Wild.

"Why me, though?"

"For the same reason the invitation was sent to you. What do you know about the Wild family history?"

I shrugged. "Well... Jesup Wild was supposed to have been an outlaw, and there are rumors that he buried a treasure somewhere in the mountains." I tipped my chin in the general direction of the mountain ranges. "But no one has ever found anything. At least, not by my family." I licked my lips, suddenly unsure about the stories that were told to me as a child. Surely someone would have found something by now if it was true, right? Or at least debunked the myth. "And Edmund was always going on and on about the Wild legacy and how I had to uphold my duty to it."

Kage picked up on my hesitation. "But you don't believe that, do you?" He leaned forward, his tattooed hands with their macabre skulls grinning at me, resting on his knees. "What if I told you the legacy that Edmund led you to believe was part of your inheritance, was actually something else? Something far older, far more notorious and dangerous than anyone would ever believe?"

"I'd say you were full of shit."

He barked a laugh, leaning forward, and there was nothing in his gaze or features that said he found any of this amusing. "Juniper, we don't know each other that well, but let me tell you something right now, little sister, I am not a liar."

"You can believe him, Juniper." Cade spoke now, his rough voice vibrating through me and I realized he'd tensed up like a coiled spring, carefully containing his emotions and thoughts. "He's many things, but never a liar. If Kage says that Edmund was broke and that there's something else at work here, you can trust what he says." His hazel eyes narrowed, and his jaw flexed as he worked through some inner thoughts. "How did you find this out?" He asked Kage.

Kage's dark eyes flicked towards Cade, and his lips curled into a wolfish smile. "Because I do my research, Cade. You should know this. This information wasn't easy to come by. It's why it took me longer than expected to get back here." There was something about the way he looked at Cade and the tone of his voice, that gave me the impression that his type of research didn't involve hitting the library or internet searches. I had a feeling it involved more blood and broken bones than asking simple questions.

My stomach roiled with anxiety. "Are you saying that Edmund made up the legacy part? But why?"

He smiled, white teeth flashing, and it wasn't pleasant. Kage Diovolo wasn't a man used to repeating himself. Well, he could just get over it. He'd clearly never had a sibling either.

"He didn't make it up, but he wasn't completely honest about it either. What's easier to make believable? An outright lie? Or a lie woven with just a hint of truth and enough guilt to make everyone involved go along with it?" Kage's black eyes pierced through me, and I tucked that bit of information away.

"And what about Cade's dad?" A black brow arched in surprise.

"David? What about him?"

"Well there was a photo and, well, here…" I reached into my jacket pocket and pulled out the photos, handing them to Kage who took them from me almost reverently, his eyes darkening when he saw the image of his father.

"Edmund hated David Black. My whole life I was told

Cade was my enemy." My eyes glanced at Cade but he didn't look at me. "And Edmund killed our father, but here they all are together, looking like they were having the time of their lives. Do you know what happened?"

A flash of something that might have been pain flitted across Kage's features, before he handed the photo's back to me. "No, not entirely. But seeing these confirms what I'm about to tell you next."

Kage leaned forward. "Like most tall tales, there's some truth to the story. The treasure that Jesup Wild hid in the mountains wasn't gold and diamonds." My temples throbbed with the pounding of my heart.

"The treasure was, and has always been the blood that flows through your veins."

"The Wild Legacy." The words felt like they were stuck on my tongue, my voice barely above a whisper, but Kage heard it and nodded.

"Yes, the Wild Legacy. Only it wasn't the "Wild" legacy. Like I said, that was something Edmund twisted to his benefit. It was your legacy and your mother's legacy, and your mother's mother before her. And that's why Edmund Wild wants control of you so badly, because without you, he gets none of it."

"And the people that sent me the invitation? Who are they? What do they want with me?" I thought back to all the times Edmund had lectured me about my role in the family, my purpose, and the legacy I needed to live up to. I thought about the manipulation. Oh god. My mother. He'd murdered my mother to have control of me. Nausea rolled through me.

"They are a secret organization known as the Infernals. It's a closed-door group that some say goes back to the times of the Templars, but no one knows anything concrete about them. Or if they do, they refuse to share." He scowled at that, as if he wasn't happy with the fact that he hadn't been able to threaten or beat the information out of anyone. "As for what they want? The same thing that Edmund wants, but for different reasons." Kage sighed and shook his head, a frown creasing between his brows. "Juniper, this is going to sound crazy." His eyes flashed with intensity as he leaned forward, my reflection dancing in their black depths. "But you have to believe me. I've been looking into these people for a long, long time. I can tell you one thing for certain. The only thing they value above their secrecy is the blood that keeps their organization going. Blood and money. And your blood is more important to them than any other. They will stop at nothing to get you back into their fold."

"My blood? What could they possibly want with my blood?" My brain was racing with images of some secret, dark society hunting me through the rocky mountains to drain my blood for some ritualistic sacrifice.

"Because *your* blood, my beautiful sister, is royal. Your bloodline can be traced back to ancient kings and queens. In fact, all the members of the Infernals can be connected in some way to a royal or noble line. It's one of the most important requirements for joining them. These are powerful, dangerous families. They make the Rothschilds and Vanderbilts look like child's play, Juniper. The only thing they care about is money, power, and ensuring it stays within their approved bloodlines." He sat back. "You are quite literally, to them, the equivalent of a long, lost princess. A princess they would very much like to get back and marry off to one of their approved matches, thus continuing the cycle and their reign of purity." His lips curled into a thinly veiled snarl of disgust and hatred.

We stared at each other from across the short distance between us for what felt like an eternity, before I tipped my head back and laughed. The laugh bubbled up from somewhere deep inside of me and continued as I stood up and made my way to the door.

Cade and Kage leapt to their feet.

"Pretty girl..."

"Juniper, where are you going?"

I opened the door, still laughing, feeling like my world was a comedy and I was the main punchline.

"My long-lost brother just told me." I held my fingers up as I ticked off the list. "My mother was murdered, my father was murdered, both by the man who I *thought* was my father, and I'm some long-lost princess wanted by sickos to be their baby-making machine. Where do you think I'm going? To the bar to get a drink."

Cade caught up to me and grabbed my arm, stopping. "Juniper, I know it seems crazy, believe me, I'm having a hard time understanding what the fuck is going on. But I know Kage. He wouldn't make this up. You need to listen to him."

Kage moved towards us. "It's ok, Cade. She has no reason to trust me. But maybe a drink isn't a bad idea. You're going to need it when I tell you the rest of the story." He glanced down at a black Hermes watch that looked like it was worth more than she made in an entire year. "But believe me when I say this, Juniper, you need to be careful. These people won't wait forever for an answer. And it's only a matter of time before Edmund makes his move. You need to be protected. No more going anywhere on your own."

I glanced between the two men and snorted. "Listen, I don't know what kind of neanderthal *Knights of Camelot* fantasy you two are living out right now, but I am more than capable of handling myself. Now, who's taking me to the bar? Or do I have to call a ride?"

Both men gave each other a look that I couldn't interpret, but I imagined that they were carrying on some silent conversation. Finally, Cade looked at me and sighed. "Come on, pretty girl, what kind of drink are you in the mood for?"

I turned on my heel. "The kind that says *your life is a fucking mess*." I jutted my chin toward my brother with a pointed glance at his watch. "Oh, and he's paying. Let's go."

16

CADE

*R*age.

Black and glittering danced on the edge of my vision. I blinked the dark spots away as I sat across the table in the dark corner booth, at the sports bar we'd found open for lunch.

The last several hours had revealed more about my past and Juniper's family than I ever wanted to know. And it terrified me.

It terrified me because these faceless people held more power in their pinky than I'd ever dreamt of having. Not that I wanted power. That was Kage's deal. I just wanted to protect Juniper, to keep her safe. And I had no clue how I was going to fucking do it.

Because these weren't the kind of low-life thugs I was used to dealing with. These were people who were evil for no reason other than believing by the right of their blood that their power, money and status were owed to them.

Juniper had ordered a tall beer, but then spent the rest of the afternoon nursing it, barely bringing it to her lips. The more Kage talked, the paler Juniper had gotten, as if with every word her energy was drained. At one point, she'd excused herself to the bathroom and it was just Kage and I, alone in the corner booth.

"You've made a mess." Kage didn't have to tell me what he was referring to. I already knew.

"You would have done the same thing." I'd sat back crossing my arms, prepared to take the reprimand, knowing full well that what I'd done to the sheriff had been nothing compared to what Kage would have done. Kage liked to play with his victims. To toy with them and break them long after he'd gotten what he wanted from them. I preferred to just end them.

He snarled. "I would have been clean about it. You were sloppy, Cade."

"So clean up the mess." I snarled back. "You weren't there. You didn't see what I saw. Edmund fucking *used* her to keep power over the sheriff. That's how he paid him. It wasn't money. It was Juniper." *It's always Juniper.* Juniper was the currency in which these sick bastards used to stay in power. I wanted to pound the sheriff's skull in all over again. "And now you're doing the same thing."

Something dark and dangerous glinted in Kage's black eyes. "Be very fucking careful with the accusations you're tossing out there, Cade."

I leaned forward, too pissed to mince my words. "I know you, Kage. You want something from Juniper. You want something from me as well and you're using her past, her family's history and your status as the long-lost brother to get it."

"And what will you do about it, Cade? Are you going to go up against these people by yourself? Are you going to let Juniper?" He sat back, a confident smirk curling at the corner of his smug mouth. "No. It doesn't matter what I want, does it? Because you need me. And you know it."

"What does he know?" Juniper was back now, a fine sheen of sweat dotting her brow. She looked like she was going to be sick.

"He knows he's a dick," I answered, before Kage could interject. Juniper slid in next to me and wrapped her hands around her warm beer glass, as if that would steady her somehow. "You okay?" I whispered, but she just shook her head ignoring my question, fixing Kage with a stubborn glare.

"Alright, let's go over this one more time."

Kage smiled as if he had the patience of a saint, but I knew better. He only had the patience of a man who was willing to do anything to get what he wanted.

"These people, the Infernals, are a secret society controlled by powerful families." Juniper paused, waiting for Kage to verify if she was correct, and when he nodded, she continued.

"Including my mother's family, Edmund's family, and possibly Cade's based on that photo I found." Another nod and she took a deep breath in. "And these people have some psychotic idea that only those of a chosen bloodline have a right to the money and power they hold."

"It's not an idea to them, Juniper." Kage leaned forward, his eyes burning with intensity. "It is a fundamental belief. They believe it is their God-given *right*. That they are divinely chosen. The way that kings and queens believed they were divinely chosen to rule. Except, when that idea was phased out with the modern invention of democracy, these people took their beliefs and went underground with them. Successfully, too. Their fortunes and empires are vast, and wealth is shared by the few families that control it."

"And now, because of my..." her nose wrinkled in disgust. "...blood, they want me to come back and be their perfect gene pool baby-making machine."

Kage nodded once more. "That's as much as I've been able to gather. I don't know the extent of their ideologies, or the way in which they spread the money between the families. It seems like some families stayed in the organization and others left." His gaze flicked to mine. "And I don't know how your Dad fits into the equation yet either. From what I gather, there's no noble or royal bloodline that can tie you back to the group. But your dad was involved in some way if that picture Juniper found is to be believed." He shook his head, obviously bothered by the puzzle. "But unless I can get access to the group, we'll never know. That's why Juniper needs to answer their invitation. It's the only way to get the answers we need."

Juniper eyed him for a moment, her mind clearly turning everything over. "I know why *I* want answers, Kage. But why do *you*? What's in it for you?"

"Because I think our father was trying to get into this group. And I think that's why he was killed." And then it dawned on me.

"You want revenge." I snarled the word and two sets of eyes—both completely different in color and yet, something about their shape and the intensity of their stares made them identical, swiveled toward me.

"Yes, Cade. I want revenge." Kage had the decency not to hide his motivations, at least. His dark gaze turned back to Juniper. "I want revenge for the both of us, and I think you want that too." Something passed between them then, a look and a silent conversation I couldn't understand. My fingers gripped the table so hard that I felt it crack beneath them.

"Juniper, it's not safe. These people are insane, and he's asking you to jump from the frying pan right into the fire with them." My heart pounded in my ears. She couldn't possibly be considering his proposal. It was as insane as the people he claimed ran this organization. Glacier blue eyes turned toward me again, and there was a moment of sympathy that passed through them, as if she could see my fear and panic.

"I don't have a choice, Cade. I was born already in the fire." She looked back at her brother and nodded. "Okay, I'm in. I'll answer their invitation, but we need a good fucking plan. And I want protection for my brother."

Kage nodded solemnly. "He'll be protected. I vow it."

"I mean starting now. Not tomorrow or sometime this week. I need to know Edmund won't be able to get access to Dean." Fierce protectiveness laced her voice and once again I was reminded of the similarity between her and the man she was sitting across from. "Bess should have Dean packed and ready to head to his new school by now," she said. "I want someone with them at all times– even at the school."

It took Kage but a moment to open his phone and send off a message. 'It's done." And I knew with those two simple words that it would be. But that didn't mean that I hadn't already made plans myself to ensure Dean would be watched over while he was away. I knew better than most how easily the boy could find trouble– whether he wanted to or not.

Juniper nodded and rubbed her temples. "Okay, well, if you'll excuse me. I think I've had enough mind-fucks for one day. And I need to say goodbye to my brother."

She slid out of the booth and I followed. I couldn't look at Kage. At the moment, I wanted to throttle him. As much as I understood the reason *why* he wanted revenge on this group, he was dragging Juniper into his personal vendetta and it pissed me off.

"Juniper, wait." Kage stopped us and he approached Juniper with a small, cloth-bound journal held in his hands. "I found it recently in some of my father's things. It's locked and I could have broken it open, but somehow that didn't feel like the right thing to do. It was your mother's. " He held it out to her. "I think he'd want you to have it."

Juniper eyed the faded, cloth-bound journal before accepting it from him with a weak smile. "Thank you, Kage."

He nodded, "I'll be in touch."

I grabbed Juniper's elbow and directed her to the front before I did something stupid, like punch my oldest friend in the face simply because I was angry over a situation I had no control over. "Come on, pretty girl. Let's get you home."

17

———

JUNIPER

The beer I'd ordered had turned sour on my tongue the minute Kage had started to speak. Somehow in my mind, I'd assumed that it couldn't get any worse than what he'd already told us. But it did.

Somehow, it fucking did.

I flopped down on my bed and tried to block out the raging storm of thoughts that threatened to send me spiraling, screaming into madness. Because that's what this all felt like. Complete and utter madness. My temples throbbed. The migraine I'd been fending off slowly crept into the edges of my visions as I blinked away the dark spots.

It hadn't helped that the goodbye with Dean had been emotional and messy. At least for me. Dean had just grimaced with typical teenage disgust as I'd held on to him and blubbered like a baby. Kage had kept his word though and a sleek, blacked out sedan, with what I was sure was bulletproof glass and a stone-faced driver pulled up our driveway as the afternoon sun was beginning to crest the mountain peaks.

Dean stopped before Cade, gripping his backpack and shifting it higher onto his shoulder, as Cade leaned down to speak to him in a low tone. I couldn't hear what he was saying, couldn't even process what was happening through the ringing in my ears and haze to my teary vision– but Dean's jaw hardened with a look of determination and he nodded solemnly, then in a surprising movement flung his arms around Cade's waist and gripped him tight. Cade hugged him back for a moment and then in the next Dean was in the car with a look that might have been worry flickering in those hazel-green eyes– and then he was gone and something in me cracked. Whatever happened to me, I knew Dean would be safe now. Edmund couldn't get to him.

Cade turned, looked at me– and immediately sent me upstairs to rest. It was the only thing he'd said to me the entire ride home. He'd been a silent, seething giant next to me, but I didn't have it in me to care. Although I couldn't understand why, it felt like he was angry at *me,* as if I was at fault for our fucked up family history.

What I really wanted was a time machine. I turned my

face and my gaze found the picture of my mother in its gilded frame. Her sunshine golden hair gleaming, her blue eyes sparkling, and a secretive smile curving her upturned lips. Secrets. So many secrets. And I'd been kept in the dark with all of them. *Why didn't you tell me, Mom?* I silently pleaded with her as tears began to form. I quickly wiped them away. Crying wouldn't do me any good now. Now, I had decisions to make.

The one thing Kage was certain of, was that if I wanted answers and the threat of Edmund gone, then I had to accept their invitation. I could choose to ignore it and pretend that my life was normal, but we both knew that while Edmund was still in the picture, that would never happen.

He'd killed our father.

He'd killed my mother.

He'd threatened my little brother.

All to control me. Me, the girl with the precious blood. I looked down at my hands as guilt ripped through me. Their blood was on my hands. And so was every other person in harm's way until he was stopped.

Who would he go after next?

Kage had revealed that the location for the meeting would be at the group's private club, Eros. A place that until now, he'd been denied access to. But with my help, now he could get in and get the answers that he so desperately sought. Answers I wanted to know as well. How had our parents met? Why did our father want in the group so badly? Was it because of my mother?

I picked up the journal that Kage had given me, my fingers running over the faded, gold lettering on the front before fingering the lock on the side. Pulling open my bedside table, I fished for the small key I'd found in my father's desk all those weeks ago, my fingers shaking as I inserted it into the lock and felt it open with a soft *click*. Opening it to the first page, I recognized my mother's handwriting immediately, holding back a sob. Skimming through the pages, I read lines of poetry, musings about the day, anticipation over upcoming events and names that were scrawled in an elegant script. The journal looked like it spanned years with some gaps missing here and there, as if she'd set it down and suddenly remembered to pick it back up again. I stopped at a date that was just a few months before I was born. There was something different in her tone and the way she wrote her words. Something more serious, more mature in the purposeful script.

April 26, 1999

It's been done. The council won't like my decision, Edmund won't like my decision. But I had to follow my heart. The line ends with me. The lies, the deceit, the innocent blood, it all ends with me. I won't let the legacy of my blood hurt any more inno-

cents. Most importantly, the innocent babe I carry. Her worth is far more than just her blood.

Decision? What decision? I flipped the page, only to be met with blank lines. Nothing. "No!" The journal was launched out of my hand before I could think, only to be met with a wall of muscle standing in my doorway as it bounced off his chest and fell to the floor. A dark brow arched over his golden-flecked eyes, and I dropped my gaze to see that Cade was standing there holding a tray with a sandwich, water and my medicine on it.

"Not sure if the book deserved that." He carefully transitioned the tray to one hand and bent down to pick up the journal.

Frustration boiled under my skin and I snapped. "No, but maybe you did. What are you doing, Cade?"

He ignored my question and moved over to where I was laying, setting the tray down on the bedside table before handing me back the journal.

"Bess made you a sandwich. She says you need to eat before you take your pill. How long have you been taking these meds?"

I grabbed the journal and tossed it—a little less carelessly, onto the bedspread next to me. "That's none of your business."

Something flickered across his gaze and he picked up the bottle, shaking it before handing it to me. "I already told you, Juniper, everything is my business where you are concerned."

I snorted, reaching for the water glass before opening up the bottle and dumping a pill into my hand. "Wrong. Everything concerning me is *only* your business if I allow it to be." Tipping my head back, I swallowed the meds and let the cool water glide down my throat. My temples throbbed, my stomach roiled. But it was going to be okay. On a scale of one-to-fucked, this migraine was somewhere around the *bitch, you're just having a bad day* scale. I could handle bad days.

I looked up at the dark cloud of a 6'4" asshole who was standing over me. Cade Black though, I couldn't handle him right now. I wasn't sure if I'd ever be able to handle him after what I'd learned today. "And I'm not sure I want to allow you into my business anymore, Cade. Not unless you can extend the same courtesy to me." If he thought for one second I'd forgotten about how he'd withheld information from me, then he was dead wrong.

His jaw flexed. The only sign that my words had their desired effect. "Things aren't as black and white as you want to paint them, pretty girl." His voice rumbled as he crossed his arms and stared down at me, as if by the force of his glare he could get me to back down.

I held his glare. "Then paint me a different picture, Cade. Because from where I'm standing, there's the world according to Cade, and then there's the truth." My fingers found my bedspread, and I bunched the fabric between my fists in an effort to center myself as the emotions threatened to spill over. "You hated me for years for a lie that I was forced to tell. Forced to perpetuate because I was just a kid who didn't know any better. But you couldn't even be honest with me about who my brother is." I blinked up at him, my gaze tracing over the scar that marred his beautiful face and the shadow of a dark beard caressing his jaw. Scanning lower to the swirl of tattoos, with their mocking skulls and dancing shadows that peeked out beneath his thermal shirt. Continuing down to his balled-up fists, with fresh cuts and bruises across his knuckles. My eyes met his again. "You can't even be honest about who you really are."

I could almost hear his teeth grinding as his jaw flexed again.

"I told you, my relationship with Kage is complicated."

"Then uncomplicate it."

"Juniper—," There was a warning edge to his voice, but I was past the point of heeding any warning signs.

"I think we're done here, Cade." I set my water glass back on my bedside table. "Thank you for taking me to meet my brother. And thank you for helping me with

Dean." The words were coming, but they felt like razor blades on my tongue. "But I don't think that we should continue…" I waved my hand at the space between us. "…this, whatever *this* is, anymore." I couldn't do it. I couldn't continue with a relationship built on lies and half-truths, no matter what excuse or validation there was for them.

He grabbed my hand, his grip vice-like and in the next instant, I was on my feet and pulled to his chest. "You don't get to do that, Juniper.' His face was inches from mine, our noses nearly touching as he growled the words making things twist and tighten low in my belly. "You don't get to waltz back into my life, flip my world upside down, then tell me how to paint you a fucking picture."

"Paint it, color it, use a fucking pencil for all I care." I held his stare. "But tell me the truth about something, Cade. How'd you really get those cuts and bruises on your knuckles?" He didn't want to talk about Kage? Fine. I wasn't entirely sure I wanted to discuss him yet, either. Whatever their history was, I'd find out in good time, but I'd had enough history lessons for one day.

His eyes went hard and he dropped my hand, stepping away from me as if it suddenly hurt to be standing so close. "I told you. You don't get to tell me how to paint a fucking picture, Juniper Wild."

Something shifted in the air, as if an invisible wall had

been slammed down between us. Or maybe we'd just finally run into it and it had been there all along, waiting for this moment.

"Then I guess everything about me isn't your business after all, is it Cade Black?"

Silence hung in the air like a guillotine for half a heartbeat and then, without a word, he turned on his heel and walked out, shutting the door firmly behind him.

For the second time in my life, Cade Black once again broke my heart.

JUNIPER

I watched without really seeing as green peas rolled around my plate, playing a sick game of dodge-the-fork that I was only half-heartedly invested in. If the pea didn't want to sacrifice itself to the end of the steel prong and prolong its slow, rotting death at the bottom of the compost pile instead, who was I to complain? It's not like I would taste it, anyway. I made to stab at the pile once more, watching as one bounced, hoping to make its escape, and instead landed in a pile of steaming mashed potatoes that were drowning in gravy. Poor little guy just couldn't catch a break.

"I'm not a fan of peas, either." A smooth voice interrupted my wild fantasy of peas forming a pea-chain to save their drowning comrade from the potato avalanche and I blushed, embarrassed I'd been caught day-dreaming. I was being rude.

I raised my gaze to meet the black-eyed stare of my brother, who was sitting across from me at the table in my formal dining room. A soft smile that seemed contradictory to the hard, angular planes of his jaw played about his lips. I returned it half-heartedly. This dinner had been my idea. After a night of restless sleep, I'd woken up to a message from Kage letting me know his office hadn't heard anything yet from Stacy and, on a whim, I'd invited him over for dinner. At the time, I had told myself that it was because I wanted to get to know him better. Despite his reputation and the rumors that swirled around about him, he was my brother. In a different life, we might have even grown up together. But in reality, it was just a distraction from the overwhelming thoughts of watching a hazel-eyed biker walk out of my life and destroy the little bit of hope I'd had for us.

"Yeah, they've never been my go-to vegetable." I wrinkled my nose. "Or mushrooms, for that matter." Maybe I needed to give up on a well-balanced diet and stick to pizza. "When I was little, my mom would tell me that my peas were laughing at me to get me to eat them." With a shake of my head, I reached for my glass of wine. Kage had brought it with him, some expensive brand that I couldn't even pronounce the name of, but it had a rich, smoky flavor with just a hint of pepper as it hit my tongue. I liked it and I wasn't even a wine drinker. Maybe I had more in common with my brother than I initially thought.

"I remember her." He murmured, his dark brows furrowed in a frown as he stared down at his plate.

"I—," My throat threatened to cut off the words. "…didn't realize you'd ever met her."

He nodded and pushed away from the table to come and refill my glass. "It's more of an impression of her than anything else. I was too young at the time to understand who she was, or her importance to him." Something glinted in the dark depths of his eyes. "But I remember he smiled a lot when he was with her."

Cocking my head, I watched as he sat back down, all elegance and grace in a black, long-sleeved button-up and designer jeans. It was at odds with what I knew lurked underneath. He'd come dressed much less formally than the designer suit and tie I was used to seeing him conduct his business in. Yet, it still screamed wealth, power and intimidation. Without realizing it, I'd sat Kage at the head of the table where Edmund used to sit, and I couldn't help but draw the comparison.

Both men were powerful, dangerous and well connected.

Both men wanted something from me.

What would happen once Kage got it, though? He didn't seem the type of man who put a lot of stock into family, especially after what he'd said about our grandfather.

"You say that like your dad didn't smile a lot before he met my mother." I took another sip of my wine, careful to not overindulge. The last thing I needed was to let my guard down completely around a man who was a known gangster and suspected killer. Brother or not.

"*Our* dad." He corrected, and my gut clenched. "And no, he didn't. Ours wasn't the type of family that spent the holidays making postcard memories." He reached for a bread roll and tore off a chunk. "He tried to shield me from it the best he could. I think dad wanted something different for me. But once he died, our grandfather stepped in and picked up where our father had slacked-off in training."

"Training? You make it sound like you were raised in a military compound." I'd stopped pretending to eat and sat back, observing everything my brother did. From the way he moved, to the way his mouth formed words, trying to get a sense of the man who fathered us both by watching the near spitting image of him sitting across from me.

White teeth glinted in the dim lighting, predatory and feral. "We are Diovolos, Juniper. Life as a Diovolo is a life of war. You are either prepared for it, or you die."

"You say that like I'm a Diovolo, too." My pulse spiked. I'd been raised my entire life to be a Wild. To be the legacy that came with that name. The idea that I could be something more, something different, sent a shockwave through me.

He shrugged, casually graceful in a way I wasn't sure I could ever be. "That is entirely up to you. I won't make demands of you." Something passed between us in the look that he gave me from across the table. Something that said he understood all too well what it was like to be forced into a life you didn't choose for yourself. It was the same feeling I got whenever I looked at Dean. Not for the first time, I wondered what it would have been like to grow up with Kage as the big brother and I, the little sister.

"What if," I cleared my throat, suddenly nervous and yet driven by the desire, the *need* to know. "...what if I wanted to find out? What if I wanted a chance to make that choice?"

He cocked his head, studying me and I wondered if he hadn't been preparing for me to ask that question all along. "You're asking me to let you see behind the curtain. This isn't Oz, Juniper. I'm not a wizard. Stepping into my world will be nothing like what you've seen so far, even when you were still Edmund Wild's daughter. And quite frankly, I'm not sure our father, or Cade for that matter, would have wanted you to even sniff at it." He leaned forward and I was met with the full force and intensity of Kage Diovolo, my brother's gaze. "But I'm not our father."

Kage's words sunk in. He wasn't our father. He was the man his grandfather, *our* grandfather, had raised. Raised to kill him and then succeed in his place. I snorted. No, Cade certainly wouldn't approve of me peeking behind the curtain into my brother's world. A world Cade was somehow a part of, but still hid from me. As if I needed to be protected from the dark like a babe needed a night light. "No, you're not. And neither is Cade. He doesn't have a say in what I do with my life."

A dark brow arched as a glimmer of amusement flashed in his eyes. "Trouble in paradise?" He purred, reaching for his wine glass, the gold rings on his fingers flashing, and my gaze was drawn to the skulls that grinned tauntingly at me. Skulls that looked eerily similar to the ones that graced Cade's arms and hands.

"There's no paradise for us. There never was." I shook my head and stared pointedly at his tattoos. "You and Cade have known each other for a long time. How did you meet?"

"What makes you think we've known each other for a long time?" Kage's smile was all pointed teeth as it stretched across his face.

"Your tattoos, for one," I rolled my eyes, annoyed at the way he so obviously tried to dodge my question. "They're almost identical. I'd even dare to say ritualistic. And two, the fact that he protects you like his life depends on it."

"Family isn't always born of blood. You could say that we grew up together, however, if Cade hasn't revealed our history then I'm sure he has his reasons for doing so." I started to interrupt, frustrated at being stonewalled once again from finding out more about Cade's past, but Kage held up a finger continuing on. "...but, since you want to know so badly about our family and what it means to be a Diovolo, maybe I can shed a little bit of light on that without revealing too many of Cade's secrets." He stood up from the table and came around to where I was sitting, pulling me out of my chair. "Get your coat," He commanded.

"Where are we going?" I blinked in confusion, as he opened up his phone and shot off a quick text message.

There was a devilish gleam in his eyes that sent goosebumps along my spine. "I have something for you, sister dear. Consider it a gift."

"A gift?" I squeaked out.

"Yes. One I think you'll find most...satisfying." The way he drew out the word and the cruel twist of his lips made my stomach drop.

I felt like I was caught in some twisted game of cat and mouse. And there was no doubt about it, I was most definitely the mouse.

19

JUNIPER

The run-down warehouse we pulled up to looked like it had been abandoned years ago. For all I'd known about my home town, this section of it was a complete mystery to me, and the unfamiliar territory didn't do much to help ease the anxious ball of nerves that was my stomach.

Kage's blacked-out Audi RS7 stood out like a sore thumb among the trash cans that were tipped over and the debris that was littered around the alley in front of the heavy, metal doors, but somehow I didn't think there would be anyone around to comment on it. The ride had been quiet, with neither one of us choosing to break the silence with idle small talk. Something I was grateful for. My nerves wouldn't have been able to keep my mouth in check, and I was sure I'd blurt out some stupid question like, *"So, who have you killed lately? Anyone I know? Are you planning on it being me?"*

Because that was what I'd been thinking from the moment I'd gotten into his car and we'd sped off into the night. I was in the car with a bona fide killer, never mind that he was my brother. His grandfather's death had proven that family ties didn't really matter much to him. If I was in the way, Kage wouldn't hesitate to remove me.

Or would he? My gaze slid to my brother as he parked the car and sent off a rapid-fire series of text messages. The skulls on his knuckles danced in the dim interior lighting, grinning at me in a way that almost made me think they were taunting me, daring me to call it off and retreat into the safe world I'd once known. Blissfully unaware of any *legacy* or danger.

Kage opened his car door and stepped out, coming around to my side and opening the door for me, his hand reaching out in invitation. I took a deep breath, my eyes fixated on his fingers and the wide expanse of his palm. This was it. This was my last chance to back away and say no. I could feel his eyes boring into me as if he knew the internal struggle I was having.

"Juniper?" My eyes flicked upward to meet his, and I was taken aback for a moment by the empathy I found in them. "You don't have to do this." He was giving me an out.

Something unclenched in my gut and I felt my breath release. I put my hand in his. "Yes, I do."

He didn't say anything else as he pulled me out of the car and shut the door behind me. The chilly air bit into my cheeks, as if the mountain weather had decided to skip fall entirely and plunge the city straight into winter. I pulled my leather jacket tighter around my midsection before following Kage across the alley to the metal doors, where one was now being held open by a tall, burly man, dressed entirely in black leather, with tattoo's covering nearly every part of his face.

Tattoo face didn't blink at me as we approached, and instead fixed his beady eyes on Kage. "He's all ready for you, sir."

Kage nodded, barely sparing the man a glance, but I couldn't help but notice the grinning skulls that decorated the right side of his face. There were three of them in total, and they looked eerily like the same skulls that graced Cade's arms and Kage's hands. I stopped short and faced him, tipping my head back to meet his eyes as he towered over me.

"Nice tats." I said.

The man blinked as if dumbfounded that a living, breathing human was actually speaking to him.

"Who did your work?" I asked, shifting slightly to the side to get a better look at the distinct shading and line-work. They were definitely done by the same artist.

Kage said nothing behind me, but I could feel his presence like a watchful, curious shadow.

Tattoo face flicked a glance to Kage as if seeking his permission before eyeing me again. "He's a private artist. No one you'd know."

"Huh…" I cocked my head, studying the way the tattoo's grinned and danced in the shadows of the dim alley light. "What do they stand for?"

He shifted, just the slightest, his face hardening for a moment. "That's club business."

"Well, considering I'm his—" I jerked my thumb over my shoulder to where Kage was standing sentinel behind me. "—sister, I guess that makes it my business too."

Again there was a quick glance of confirmation to Kage, but I held up my hand. "Uh-uh, eyes over here, big boy. I'm asking the questions, not him." Tatty-face's eyes jerked back down to meet mine, his mouth opening in shock at my boldness, and at the fact that Kage said nothing to counter my demands.

"They stand for kills. Each skull is a mark of death." He blurted out, before looking worriedly at Kage once more. "Oh shit, sir…" But Kage kept his gaze intently on me.

"It's alright, Marco. Bossiness runs in the family."

My stomach clenched, and I knew my face had gone at least two shades paler, but I didn't say anything, just nodded my head and murmured my thanks before heading inside the dark interior of the warehouse. Kage followed behind me. "Juniper..." He murmured in the dark.

I stopped short to catch my breath and tamp down on the rising nausea. Each skull stood for a kill. A death. My brother's hands were literally death.

And so were Cade's. His arms were covered in dozens of grinning, sardonic skulls. I'd laid there admiring the beautiful way they twisted, danced and teased at me out of their veils of smoke and shadow. I hadn't even been able to count them all because each time I thought I had a number, a new one would peek out at me from where it was half-hidden in shadow.

I felt Kage take my elbow, and it took everything in me not to jerk it away and run screaming. "You had that guy standing out there on purpose." I hissed at him.

His face was impassive. Those black eyes like deep pits daring me to fall into their darkness. "I knew that you needed answers to questions, and Cade isn't prepared to give them to you right now." There was almost a hint of apology in his voice, as if he felt just a little bit bad about how he'd set me up.

Answers that Cade would never have given me on his

own. I knew that now, without a shadow of a doubt. Cade would have never revealed the truth about his past and who he was, because to do so would expose me to the darkness in himself. Darkness that he didn't want to face.

"Who did he kill?"

Kage held a hand to his heart in a mock protest as a smirk curved his lips upward. "Really? You're more concerned about Cade? You're not even going to question *my* markings?"

I scoffed. "Your reputation precedes you, I didn't need to know. I would have been shocked if you *didn't* have blood on your hands." My previous morbid fantasy about my brother spilling my blood on these streets flashed through me. "Unless, of course, you're planning on adding my skull to your trophies."

His smirk turned into a full grin as he let out a soft chuckle, and the tightness in my chest loosened. Kage wasn't trying to hide who he was from me. My brother embraced his darkness. Yeah, he was a manipulative bastard. What man in power wasn't? But he wasn't hiding it. Something like admiration bloomed. I'd been kept shadowed and in the dark so long by the people in my life, that seeing someone unapologetic about who and what they were was refreshing, even if it scared the living shit out of me.

"You didn't answer my question. Who did he kill? And why?"

A black brow arched in admonition. "Come on now, Juniper, you're smarter than that. *I* never said Cade killed anyone."

I glared at him. "Culpability." He wouldn't—no, *couldn't* answer my questions, because to do so would frame not only himself, but Cade as well. He was protecting him while also trying to help me. Answers to those questions weren't going to come from my brother.

We were moving now down a long corridor that was lit only by the occasional swinging lightbulb. I passed by doors that opened to long, abandoned admin offices and supply closets, but Kage kept leading me deeper and deeper into the back until we came to another set of doors leading to a stairwell. Our footsteps echoed off the metal steps as we went down to what I assumed was the basement of the building before pausing before another set of large metal doors.

Whoever or whatever was down here, was kept so far away from the outside world that no one would ever hear them scream. Anxiousness made the palms of my hands sweat, and I rubbed them on my jeans.

"You don't have like, men with machine guns behind that door waiting to shoot my head off, do you?" My nervous attempt at a joke left my voice squeaking off the metal and concrete that surrounded us in the stairwell. I didn't really believe that my brother was out to kill me, not that he wasn't completely capable, but the suspense of this surprise was beginning to weigh on my already fragile nerves. The one thing I was grateful for, whether it was the lingering effects of my medicine or not, was that my normal stress-induced headache hadn't made an appearance.

Kage's lips turned down and he turned to face me, a seriousness in his black gaze piercing through me. "Juniper, you have nothing to fear from me. I promise."

I released an anxious breath and nodded. "You're going to have to forgive my jumpiness. I'm still getting used to the idea that *the* Kage Diovolo is my brother."

"Well," There was a rumble of rough emotion in his voice. "...believe it or not, I'm still getting used to the idea of you as well." He shook his head. "I'd been told you existed, but the details of your birth were always a mystery to me. I'd honestly given it up to rumor before I was suddenly left without the best bar manager I'd ever had at the Pit."

I laughed. "You mean the only one that actually stuck around despite how hard the jackals tried to run her off."

He grinned, white teeth flashing in the dimness. "That too. I should have known then that a Diovolo had them by their balls. Now, little sister, would you like to see the gift I have for you?"

I cocked a brow. "It's a little early for Christmas and too late for my birthday."

He pushed open the door and stood back so that I could enter the warehouse. It was entirely empty except for a lone figure seated in the center of the room. I squinted in the darkness, trying to make out who was waiting for me as we approached.

I came to a dead stop several feet from the ominous figure hunched over in the chair, while Kage made his way to where the person was sitting and hadn't said a word or moved.

A gasp left my lips as ice flooded my veins when I realized why. The man's hands and legs were bound to the chair, his head covered by a black bag so that I couldn't see his face. An eerie sense of déjà vu came over me, and I looked at Kage who was resting his hand casually on the man's shoulder, watching me intently.

"You're gifting me…a person?" My voice squeaked out, and I winced at how nervous I sounded. Not at all like the sister of a bad-ass gangster.

"You haven't been very honest, Juniper." My head snapped up to meet my brother's gaze, apprehension making my stomach do small flips. There was something off about the way the man was leaning forward, his hands placed on his knees. My eyes traveled down and I noticed that he didn't have shoes on either, his feet covered by dingy socks. Why did I feel like there was something I was missing?

"What do you mean?" I asked.

"You were supposed to report to Cade if there was anything unusual going on, weren't you?" Kage's fingers gripped the shoulder they rested on, and a low moan emitted from beneath the bag. I slid a few steps closer, trying to figure out who the person was, and why I felt a sense of familiarity.

"There's been a lot of unusual things going on lately, you're going to have to be more specific than that." I retorted dryly, and somewhat proud of myself for not running away screaming. *There we are, now you're sounding like a badass.*

"Well, let's start with the skulls—"

"Cade already knew about my car." I cut him off, and Kage clicked his tongue almost as if he was scolding me.

"Juniper, you know damn well I'm not talking about your car. But fine, if you want to play coy, be my guest. I just thought you'd want a chance to ask the person responsible about all the mysterious things going on around your house." He grinned and slipped the black bag from the man's head, and my mouth dropped as I took in the bruised and bloodied face of the man that was clinging to consciousness in front of me.

A man I knew very, very well.

Anxiousness slipped away as shock and rage took over when the man blinked bleary, baby-blue eyes in my direction, giving the barest hint of recognition before closing once more in pain and groaning softly.

My brother had just gifted me my douche-bag ex. Jax Myer.

20

JUNIPER

axon—fucking—Myer, shithead ex-boyfriend extraordinaire, sat in front of me.

Or at least, what remained of him. Kage had quickly explained that Cade had known all along that there had been people tracking my movements around Wild, and having reported back to him about what he'd seen, my brother had made it his personal mission to figure out exactly who was responsible.

Apparently, a bottle opener to the balls hadn't been enough for Jax to get the message to leave me the hell alone. I glared at the man I'd thought I'd left back in Wild, noting his disheveled appearance and the hollow look to his cheeks. Life hadn't been kind to Jaxon since I'd last seen him.

"You took his toes?" I waved my hand to his feet. What I'd initially thought was just dirty socks, turned out to be dried blood from missing toes that had been severed. Jax's hands were similarly dismemberment, with several fingers still intact but only up to the second or third joint. "And his fingers?"

Kage shrugged and sent a feral grin in my direction. "I had a lot of birthdays to make up for."

"Remind me to avoid Christmas presents from you," I murmured, before I slid my booted foot forward and nudged one of the bloodied stumps. Any trepidation and fear I'd felt earlier was gone.

"Hey jackass, wake up."

Jax's blonde head rolled back as he cried out in pain, and for a moment, I felt a twinge of sympathy. But then I remembered the gun I'd kept next to my bed and the terror I'd felt every morning staring at the fresh footprints outside my window, and quickly clamped down on the emotion. Jaxon deserved nothing but my wrath.

Blood-shot blue eyes squinted at me. "June…" he groaned my name through bloodied lips and, from the sound of it, a few missing teeth as well. "June, he's crazy… get…away…"

I cocked my head to the side, my lips pursing in question. "Jax, you're literally missing parts of your anatomy and the first thing you do is accuse my brother of being crazy?" I shook my head. "I think you have much bigger things to worry about right now."

"June…" He groaned, and tried to lean forward. "you don't understand…"

"No, Jaxon, *you* don't understand." I scooted my chair closer until I could see directly into his eyes. "You think Kage is the crazy one? Just because he snipped off a couple of your fingers and toes?" I snorted. "You stalked me outside of my house, Jax. You left creepy as fuck notes and pictures. You invaded my space and *threatened* my baby brother." With every punctuated sentence, Jaxon's eyes grew wider and wider, his eyes flickering rapidly between me and Kage, who was standing nonchalantly at my back. I held out my hand and without even asking, Kage placed a set of gardening shears in them, the steel blades caked in blood. I glanced down at the handle and then back at my brother.

"Did you get these out of my shed?" I blinked at him, my brows arched in question.

He shrugged. "Seemed fitting."

I studied the blades and looked back up at my brother. "Did you also happen to bring a shovel?" He only grinned, his white teeth glinting dangerously in the shadows.

I turned back to Jax and held up the sheers. "Make no

mistake, Jaxon. You're not leaving this warehouse alive. But how many pieces you go out in is entirely up to you."

The remaining color drained from Jax's face.

"Juniper, I'm sorry. I'm so sorry." He blubbered, tears streaming down his face, leaving streaks in the blood and dripping pink onto his already stained t-shirt. "He made—he made me do it…"

"Who made you? Kage?"

Jax shook his head. "No, your father."

Understanding dawned. "He's the one who sent you to the bar that night." Memories of the tattooed men and Jaxon's insistence that I'd been keeping a secret from him, flooded back. He'd known about me, but more than that, he knew about the legacy.

He nodded. "I'm sorry, June—I didn't think…I didn't know…"

"What did he offer you? Money?" I took the bloodied tips of the shears and dragged the metal down Jax's tear-soaked face. "Power?"

Wide-eyed, Jax tried to follow where the metal touched his skin, but I tapped him gently on the cheek, bringing his attention back to me. "He offered me a chance to get in." He whispered through his bloodied and cracked lips.

"Get in where?"

"To the Infernals—to the bloodline." Jax gasped as his words caused me to lean forward enough that the sharpened ends of my shears pressed into the skin of his cheek, causing more blood to weep.

"What do you know about the Infernals?" Kage's voice was rough, dark, and filled with the promise of more pain if Jax didn't answer his question honestly.

"Enough. I know enough." Jax looked at me, his blue eyes blazing. "I didn't know you were the key, though. All that time I was fucking the goddamned *heir, and* I didn't even know it."

I shoved the shears into his crotch, and Jax let out a high-pitched shriek. "Well, you know it well enough now, dickhead. Why did Edmund think that he'd be able to get you into the Infernals? You aren't part of the bloodline."

Jax was straining, trying to pull his body as far away from me and my gardening tool of death as he could. "Through life and death! Infernal through life and death! Complete the circle! Join the blood!" He screamed.

He was clearly delusional and not making sense. You could join through life and death? What the fuck did that mean? I pulled the shears back and looked over my shoulder at Kage as Jax collapsed in relief, still muttering something about life, death and blood.

"Any idea what he's referring to?"

Kage's dark eyes narrowed. "I have some theories." His face was a dark mask of secrets. He certainly knew something, but was not willing to share yet. My gaze slid back to Jax, whose eyes had closed, either from pain or blood loss. I wasn't sure which. I also didn't really care.

"Where's Edmund?" I pulled back on the shears just enough to give Jax a momentary reprieve. He blinked his eyes and shook his head.

"I don't know."

I sighed and shoved them back into his crotch. He screamed. "I don't know! I swear, I don't! The last time I saw him he shot me, then sent me back to spy on you. He's crazy, Juniper. He's fucking crazy."

I let off again with the shears. "You listen to me, Jaxon, and listen good. You're going to cut the bullshit and start giving me some fucking answers, or I'm going to let my brother here continue dissecting you piece by fucking piece. Do you understand me?"

He was gasping now. "I mean it, Juniper. I don't know. I'll answer anything you want, I swear!"

"Fine. Why have you been following me?"

"He told me to. He told me to watch you and to see if *they* contacted you. And at first that's all I did. But then..." He took a deep breath and continued on. "...but then something made him desperate. Something made him upset. He said I needed to get you out of Wild. That you were too protected there."

"So you were trying to scare me away?" He nodded.

"At first it was with the skulls. But then you got the invitation, and he got even more upset—,"

"So you started leaving notes and stalking my property and my brother?" The pieces were clicking into place. All this time I'd thought that the Infernals were the ones who wanted me scared. But it was Edmund. It was always Edmund.

Fear radiated from Jaxon, but it was nothing compared to the complete rage I felt. "He…he wanted me to take him, if I could."

It took everything in me not to shove the metal tip into his eyeball at the sound of his confession.

"But I couldn't, because he was always with that guy. Or that guy was always around, watching you."

"Guy? What guy?" I frowned, trying to make sense of what he was telling me.

"The big muscle guy. The one with the skulls on his arms. He said he must be your new champion." His cracked lips began bleeding again with every word he spoke, and I watched as the red liquid dripped down his chin.

Cade. Cade had been there, even when I'd thought he'd

kept away. He'd watched over us. Protected us. *What did he mean by champion?*

"But then I heard you talking to Stacy…"

"Stacy?" My head snapped up, and I leaned in closer. "What do you mean you heard me talking to Stacy?"

"I was there. Outside your window. I heard you ask her to get a meeting with Kage, and I remembered how she was always butting her little punk nose into our business." He spat the last out with a sneer, blood spraying with the spittle, as I tried to wrestle with the icy dread that filled me.

"What did you do with Stacy, Jaxon?" My voice was soft, barely above a whisper, as I fought to maintain control.

He shifted nervously in his seat and then shook his head. "Fuck it, I'm not getting out of here alive anyway, so what does it matter? I told him if he wanted you to leave Wild, then he needed to get to her."

"Kage?" I couldn't see anything but Stacy's face. Her dancing, brown eyes, purple hair and piercings that somehow brought out her delicate beauty. I couldn't hear anything but her voice in my head telling me to be careful. Telling me she missed me.

"Yes, Juniper?" Kage's voice was a dark rumble of death at my back.

"Get whatever you can out of him. And then make the pieces really fucking small."

I didn't get up, didn't move an inch as Kage moved in and took the gardening shears from me. I wanted to watch and remember every single sound Jaxon made while my brother proved exactly why he was called *the Diablo.*

But I'd make the devil himself look like a daydream if Edmund Wild harmed one hair on my friend's head.

21

CADE

"75…76…77…" I huffed, my abs straining as I counted out my sit-ups on my living room floor. I was on my third round after finishing a heavy workout session in the garage gym below me.

My townhome was mid-distance between the shop and the historic part of Wild, in a newer district that had been built up within the last five years. Another gift from Kage after he'd found out I was perfectly content sleeping on the couch at the shop. I'd tried to explain to him I'd looked at multiple apartments and homes, but every time I set foot in one, all I could see was the nine-by-five prison cell that I'd spent all those years in, closing in on me. He'd handed me the keys and said I would never be able to leave that cell in my mind if I didn't first leave it with my body.

In time, I understood what he meant. I no longer saw the gray walls whenever I closed my eyes. Or felt the slamming of barred doors behind me. But there were still some things that I couldn't let go of. Like finishing a workout the way I'd done every day that I'd spent in that cell, by pushing my body to the point of exhaustion with push-ups and sit-ups until I nearly passed out. Sometimes it was the only thing that cleared my mind.

The sound of my security system alerting me to someone at my door pulled me out of my thoughts, and I set my phone back down, determined to ignore it until I caught a glimpse of blonde hair the color of gold-spun sunshine on the security camera feed.

What was Juniper doing here?

She buzzed again, and I realized I'd been staring at her on my screen instead of answering her. I hit the button and buzzed her up before walking into my kitchen to make a protein shake.

Juniper appeared around the corner a moment later, and I had to catch my breath. Somehow, the sight of her standing in my home shifted something inside of me. Her wide, blue eyes took everything in. From the modern kitchen that faced an open-concept living room, to the circular stairs that led to a loft-style bedroom area. Everything was open and I had a free line of sight from every corner of the house. Kage had done a good job picking a space that didn't make me feel like the walls were closing in on me. Even the windows that lined most of the living room wall faced the towering mountains as a backdrop to the city, so that I could see the lights and modern sprawl that spread out before them.

"Wow." She cleared her throat after a moment. "You have a really nice place." There was a stiffness in her words, a distance that I hated hearing. But I'd put it there, hadn't I? I'd slammed the door closed between us when she'd asked me for the one thing I couldn't give her. The truth.

"Thanks." I squeezed my shaker bottle and inwardly cussed at myself. One word? Really? That's all I could get out? I sounded like the neanderthal she said I was.

Clearing my throat, I waved awkwardly at the living room and the large modular couch that took up most of the space. "Do you want to sit down?"

She opened her mouth to answer, then closed it again shifting uncomfortably and shook her head. "No...I..."

Something was wrong. I could see the worry and fear in her eyes. I stepped around my kitchen island to stand in front of her. "Juniper, what's wrong? What happened?"

"He took her, Cade." Her voice trembled, tears welling in her blue depths, and something inside of me snapped.

My fingers dug into the soft leather of the jacket she wore as I closed the distance between us and grabbed her arms. "Who took her? Who are you talking about, Juniper?"

The words tumbled out of her, spilling like the tears that fell down her cheeks. "Kage took me to his warehouse. I saw Jax there. I know, Cade. I know everything. I know about the tattoos. I know about the Diablos. I know about how you spied on me."

My gut clenched as rage spiked. Fucking Kage. Of course he wouldn't waste an opportunity to pull Juniper deeper into his schemes. "What do you mean Kage showed you the warehouse? Why the fuck did you go with him?"

My anger leaked into my voice and Juniper responded by jerking out of my grip. "Because I asked him to!" She snapped. "Because he's the only person who's at least been honest with me. Yeah, he's a fucking murderer and probably more than a little on the unhinged side, so I'm not exactly sure what that says about me since he's my goddamn brother and we have the same damn DNA." She took a deep breath before shoving at my chest with her finger. "But he doesn't hide who he is from me." Those blue eyes that I wanted to drown in looked up at me, not full of anger or rage like I'd expected, but instead, they radiated with pain and regret. "He also doesn't protect me from the shadows. Or care if my car has the right tires. Or pay for my brother's school just to keep him out of trouble."

She stepped in closer and placed a hand on my chest, just over my heart. "He didn't tattoo my art on his chest. Or remember how I take my coffee." My breath caught as I fought the urge to lean down and inhale her honeyed scent. To breathe her in so deep that she was permanently etched into my soul.

"My brother doesn't hide who he is from me because he doesn't care about shielding me. Either I'll survive, or I won't." She chuckled, half a smirk curving her beautiful lips, even as the tears still streaked down her cheeks. "And I'm ok with that. I really am."

She took a deep breath and continued on. "So you can be mad at Kage for opening my eyes to the darker aspects of his life all you want. But you have to understand something. It's my choice if I want to step into it. I'm not afraid of the dark, Cade." Her head tipped back and her gaze pierced my soul. "I'm not afraid of you."

"You should be, pretty girl." It was my turn to step away from her. I lifted my hands up, brandishing the cuts and bruises on them. "You don't know the things I've seen, the things I've done, or the lengths I would go to protect you." I dropped my hands to my sides once more, but before they could fall, she reached out and snatched them into her grip.

"You mean like taking out the sheriff?"

My jaw flexed, and images of punching Kage in his big, fat fucking mouth flashed through my brain. "He told you?"

She shook her head. "He didn't need to. I put two and two together after the visit to the warehouse, and Jax gave up the name of the person helping to track me."

She dropped my hands and held her own out. "You think you're the only one with dark secrets? My scars may not be visible like yours, but they're there if you would open up your eyes and look. If you would just listen to me when I speak."

Realization came to me like a punch to the gut. Juniper knew about the photos.

"Juniper I—" but she held up a hand and cut me off.

"I don't want your pity, Cade." Her blue eyes welled with tears again that she blinked away. "You already gave me the greatest gift when you took out the son of a bitch for me."

"How long?" My voice almost broke. Visions of the sheriff's mangled face danced in my head, and I wanted to dig him up just to drown myself in his blood once again.

She shook her head. "It doesn't matter. What's done is done. What does matter is that Edmund has Stacy, my best friend. And if he's taken her, then who knows who else he's willing to go after to get to me?" The look of wild fear in her eyes told me she was already thinking of everyone who was close to her. Her friends from the Emporium, and her brother.

She gripped my arm again and tipped her head back to stare deep into my eyes. Those brilliant blues seeking mine, searching, asking, but more than that…accepting. She didn't question the murder. She didn't push me to tell her why or judge me. "I need you Cade. I need the real you. The one you try to hide from me. The one you tried to hide when we were just kids. I needed you then and I need you now. But just like it's my choice to stay or walk away from the dark, it's your choice too. I'm not going to manipulate you like my brother would. But if we're going to survive what's coming, we have to be honest with each other." She stepped in closer, and the honey and lavender scent of her washed over me once more. "You're not the person I need protecting from. You're the man I love."

Her confession slammed into me like a freight train. My fingers found her chin as I tipped her head back further, my large body caging her smaller one. She loved me.

Her words from the other night under the bleachers came back to me. *I was corrupted long before I ever met you.*

She'd been trying to tell me all this time. All those years ago she'd been trying to show me who she really was, and I'd blindly ignored it. But she'd seen me. She'd known who I was all along and accepted me.

She loved me. All of me.

The urge to protect her, to shove her in a vault while I handled whatever evil doings Edmund had planned was overwhelming. But that's not what she was asking me to do.

She loved me. She knew I had killed for her. Stole for her. Lied to and manipulated her. And she loved me.

She didn't want a knight in shining armor. She didn't want the rich daddy's friend. She wanted the killer. She wanted the man with blood on his hands. She wanted me. And I was going to give him to her. No more hiding who I was just to protect her.

"Juniper…" My head bent down, my hands moving to cradle her face.

"Yes, Cade?" Our breaths mixed as our mouths barely brushed against each other, lips tingling with the contact.

"I love you, too."

Her eyes lit up as a gasp fell from her lips, and she tried to push forward to press her mouth against mine, but I pulled away. "I love you, pretty girl. But right now? I'm going to fuck you like I don't."

22

JUNIPER

Heat flooded through me.

When Jaxon screamed out the sheriff's name during Kage's interrogation, cold rage had replaced the gut-wrenching fear I'd felt over Stacy's abduction.

The fucking sheriff.

I should have known. It was no mistake that he'd been the one to show up at the bar that night in Denver to tell me about Edmund's death. It had been no mistake that he'd made it known, in no uncertain terms, that I had to come back home to Wild.

Disgust made the bile in my stomach churn, as a splitting headache threatened to bear down on me.

I should have killed him. I should have done it the minute he appeared outside my bar.

Cade had wondered if the sheriff was being paid to

feed Edmund information, well I knew it to be true. I'd known it until I'd turned old enough to fight back and refused to be the payment for his sick deeds. That's when Edmund started using my brother as leverage to get me to do what he wanted. He couldn't control my body anymore, so he controlled me in other ways.

The pictures had started shortly after my mother died. When Kage had revealed that Edmund might have had her murdered and why, part of me already knew the answer. What better way to hide a murder than to have the sheriff in your back pocket? I should have demanded that the photos were burned. I should have exposed the sheriff for who he was. A disgusting man who preyed on the innocent instead of helping them.

But I couldn't, because it would have left Dean exposed.

So I'd left Wild and left that girl behind with it. The woman that came back didn't let the past control her anymore. No matter the lingering effects and the headaches that the trauma brought with it.

'Post-traumatic stress disorder', the free clinic volunteer psychologist had said, when I'd finally gone in for testing and no one could figure out why my migraines were so bad.

Did I know who did it? Yes.

Did I want to press charges? No.

It didn't matter. I was gone. Dean was safe.

And I had an entire file drive secured away with enough proof to put the sheriff away for life three times over. That had been my insurance policy for when I left. Edmund couldn't touch Dean, because then they both would burn.

But then Cade had discovered my secret and killed the sheriff for me. I realized as much during Jaxon's confession, and the images of Cade's bloodied and cut up hands flashed into my mind. Cade had gone to question the sheriff himself after I'd mentioned it. He'd once again stepped in between me and the darkness. He'd protected me. He'd killed for me.

When Kage was finally done and had exhausted all possible information from Jaxon, we'd left his broken and bloodied body, and headed back into the night.

He'd brought me to Cade's townhome at my request with just one piece of information. "He's not trying to lie to you, Juniper. He's trying to protect you from himself."

And then he'd sped off into the night to leave me to face off with all 6' 4" of brooding asshole.

A brooding asshole that had been standing in his kitchen, a fine sheen of sweat over his muscled frame, and dark, gray sweatpants hanging dangerously low over his hips when I'd come up the stairs and entered his home.

I hadn't really known what I was going to say once I'd

gotten there. *Thank you* seemed too casual. *Fuck me now, please*—seemed too brazen. It wasn't until I saw the pain and uncertainty in his eyes that I'd finally understood what Kage had meant.

Cade couldn't accept the darkness in himself, because he didn't think I ever would.

The words had poured out of me. Stacy was gone, and I needed him. I needed Cade. All this time, I thought I could handle Edmund on my own, but I was wrong. Just like all this time, he thought he could change who he was for me, but he was wrong. We needed each other if we were going to survive what was coming.

And what was coming was nothing short of a war.

"I love you, Cade Black." I watched as my words cracked the walls he'd built up around himself, and they came tumbling down as he finally realized the truth. I was not afraid of the dark. I was not afraid of him.

Desire burned through me as he pulled me to him, heat blazing from his body where my hands gripped firm muscles and slid over sweat-soaked skin. His mouth enveloped mine, and it was like he was inhaling me, devouring me, owning every single inch of me.

He was going to tear me apart, and I was going to let him. My nails raked down his back, and he hissed as I practically tried to climb his tall frame, grinding myself against him. His hands gripped my ass, lifting me, and I locked my legs around his waist as he carried me up the stairs to his bedroom and dropped me on the bed.

"Strip." He growled the command, and I didn't have to be told twice. His thumbs hooked under the waistband of his sweats and as he tugged them down, his thick cock sprang free. My mouth and other parts of me watered at the sight, and I sank down to my knees as he fisted the thick length in front of my face.

"Is this what you want, pretty girl?" He rubbed the tip against my lips, painting them with the pre-cum that was leaking from it, and I licked it like the delicacy it was with a moan. "You want to be my dirty girl? To worship my cock while I pray to your pretty pussy?"

I answered by opening my mouth, as he slid his length past my lips and down my throat until my eyes watered. Then he pulled out and did it again. He hissed. "God, your mouth is perfect. So fucking perfect. Do you know how many nights I used to get off thinking about ruining your fucking throat?"

He shoved his cock in again, gripping my head and holding me still as he fucked my mouth and throat. "Eyes up here, Juniper. You told me you can handle my darkness. We're about to find out." His foot nudged my legs apart and I moaned around the thick length in my mouth. "Play with your pussy and show me how wet that cunt is for me."

My fingers drifted down to where my legs were spread wide for him, my thighs glistening with wetness, and I moaned again when my fingers found my clit and began to dance around it.

"That's it. Fuck yourself on your fingers. But don't come. Those orgasms are mine."

He'd never spoken to me like this before. He'd been bossy and demanding, but the dirty words had always seemed to dance just on the edge, never spilling over into the filthy way he growled at me now. He gripped my hair harder and began to fuck my mouth in earnest. His abs bunched and flexed as his cock swelled in my mouth, burying himself down to the hilt. My eyes watered as I was forced to choke. Meanwhile, I matched his pace as I furiously fingered my dripping cunt in time to his thrusts. I was close, so close. Stars danced behind my eyes, but then he pulled me off of him with a growl.

"What did I tell you, pretty girl?" He fisted his cock, pumping the spit-soaked length over and over as jets of come splashed out and landed on my neck and chest. "Your orgasms are mine."

I whined in protest as he pulled me to my feet and pushed me back toward the bed, where I landed with a bounce. "Cade…" but he cut me off.

"Listen to me, Juniper. I'm going to fuck you. I'm going to use you. I'm going to own every inch of you." He unceremoniously flipped me to my stomach and pulled me back to the edge of the bed, where he shoved his still-hard cock inside me without warning. The stretch and burn as his thickness filled me, had me panting as I tried to push back and take him deeper. But he propped a knee up next to me, grabbed my hands and pinned them to my back, stopping me. "And when I'm done, I'm going to have you coming so hard you won't remember your own name."

He was in control. Complete and total control as he worked his length in and out of me, like he was imprinting himself permanently inside of me. Over and over again, he brought me to the edge of orgasm before denying me with a quick pinch to my clit, or moving me into a different position where I'd sob in frustration and need before he was sliding home inside of me once more.

My hands roamed my body, cupping my breasts as they bounced with every thrust while he had me on my back now, my legs thrown over his shoulders. I slid them down my stomach to my aching center as I heard myself begging for release. "Please…please Cade…"

His eyes were locked on to where we were joined, watching as his hips rolled into mine and his cock sank deeper into my heat. "You have the prettiest pussy, Juniper. You were made to take me, pretty girl."

"That's it." He growled, as he noticed my fingers

dipping into the dripping mess that was my pussy. "Spread yourself for me. Let me watch you come apart."

"Come for me now, pretty girl." He commanded, with another deep thrust of his hips.

I shattered as the tips of my fingers just barely grazed the sensitive bud, and he timed his thrusts to roll into each quiver as I barreled headlong into the orgasm that he'd denied me all night.

In the next moment, he pinned my legs to my chest as I screamed his name, pistoning in and out in a punishing rhythm as he fucked into me. "Yes, squeeze my cock, pretty girl. Fucking hell. I'm going to come inside you, Juniper, and you're going to take all of it. All of me.' He groaned and slammed home deep inside of me, filling me to the brim as he pressed me to the bed.

We stayed like that, our breathing heavy and chests moving in sync as my heart pounded in my ears, and my eyelids fluttered with the aftershocks. Ever so slowly, Cade shifted off of me and pulled me to him, my head resting on his chest where I listened to his heartbeat, strong and solid in my ear. As my eyes softly closed, heavy with sleep, I drifted away into the peaceful, dreamless darkness.

And in the dark, with Cade, I was finally home.

23

JUNIPER

Jawoke to the smell of bacon and the sound of movement coming from the kitchen below Cade's loft bedroom. Glancing over at the alarm clock on his bedside table, the red numbers blurred into focus, letting me know it was three in the morning. What was he doing making breakfast so early in the morning?

Rising from the warmth of his bed, I felt around until I found a discarded t-shirt draped carefully over the back of a chair, and slipped it on. It nearly fell to my knees and smelled like he'd recently worn it as the musky, amber scent that was uniquely his washed over me.

Padding down the spiral stairs from his loft area, I approached him quietly as he worked. He was once again dressed in gray sweatpants and shirtless, with just a kitchen towel thrown over his shoulder. Sliding onto a stool at his kitchen island, I rested my chin in my hands and admired the view. His tattoos moved and bunched over his muscles as he worked, dicing vegetables and cracking eggs. Scars I'd never noticed before stood out to me. One on his ribs, where it looked like something jagged had caught the skin and ripped. Another one in his lower back, just shy of the kidney and circular in shape. An ice-pick maybe? Or a bullet?

How many scars did he have that I'd never noticed before? That I'd never taken the time to notice?

With seamless ease, he placed all of the ingredients into a pan, grabbed a coffee mug that was filled to the brim, and slid it toward me.

"Morning sleepy-head." His smile was dazzling, and for the first time, I saw a lightness to him that made my heart melt.

"Morning? It's three a.m., what normal person is up making breakfast at three in the morning?" I sniffed at the coffee and was greeted with the scent of my favorite French vanilla creamer.

"Not a morning person, I take it?" He winked at me and turned back to the stove, where he pulled off a few strips of bacon and added more to the sizzling pan. I reached across the counter to snatch a piece where it was cooling, and took a bite with a delighted moan.

"No, but if this is how you wake me up every morning, I could be persuaded to become one."

"Make noises like that again and I might have to take you back to bed." He leaned across the counter and placed a soft kiss on my lips before snatching the rest of the bacon out of my hand. "And no snacking until it's ready."

"But!" I eyed the bacon with a pout as he placed it back on the cooling platter and sighed. "Fine, your kitchen, your rules I guess."

"It's always my rules, pretty girl." He shot me another wink before flipping the omelet onto a plate and sliding it in front of me. "But I promise it's worth the wait."

I took a bite, and the flavor exploded in my mouth. "My god, Cade, this might be better than sex."

"Say that again and I'm definitely taking you back to bed." He eyed the forkful of omelet with a jealous glare as it was headed to my mouth, like he might seriously consider snatching it away, and I quickly pulled my plate closer to me and shot him a glare.

"Don't you dare. I don't care what time of the morning it is. If I get to wake up to this, then I'm never leaving." I said, and shoved the forkful into my mouth.

"You aren't leaving, anyway." He said with a smirk, as he turned back to the stove and pulled his own omelet off the pan and onto a plate before sitting down across from me.

"Oh?" I arched a brow as I watched him eat. Everything about this seemed so cozy. So normal, despite the weight of a murderous cult and my psychopath ex-father hanging over our heads. Cade didn't even look up at me and just shrugged.

"You can't go back to your house, it's compromised. Here is the safest place for you." Something about the way he made that statement didn't settle with me.

"Jaxon is dead. The sheriff is dead. What do you mean, my house is compromised?" I asked, and took another sip of my coffee, hoping the caffeine would clear the fogginess in my head.

"Juniper." Cade's hazel and gold eyes were serious, the playfulness from earlier, gone. "Do you really think killing the sheriff and Jaxon will stop Edmund from trying to get to you again? He's already proven that he can get to you wherever you are. The only way to truly protect you is to have you either locked up in one of Kage's safe houses, or with me."

I gripped my mug and frowned. "I don't care about Edmund coming after me. I *want* him to! It's the only way we're going to get Stacy back. I'll never be safe until Edmund is dead and you'll never get him to come out in the open without me." I had no idea where Stacy was being held, or what Edmund would do to her. Either Jaxon had been more loyal to Edmund than anticipated, or he simply hadn't known, but he couldn't give us any details beyond that Edmund had her.

Cade seethed as he leaned forward and growled in a voice that left no room for argument. "It will be over my dead body if you think I'm going to allow you to use yourself as bait, Juniper Wild." Then he shoved away from the counter and began to clean up the breakfast mess. Tension settled into his muscles as anger radiated from him.

No. Not anger. Fear.

"Kage already talked to you about it." I didn't ask a question. It was a statement. Kage and I had discussed the next steps on the drive back from the warehouse. It was clear that our only option to get Stacy back and to lure Edmund out in the open, was to offer me in exchange. The only unknown in our plan was that Edmund had not reached out to me yet, and we had no idea what his next move might be. But that also meant that he might not be aware that we already knew Stacy was gone. And that could work in our favor, but only if I was the bait.

"Yeah, and I told him he could go fuck himself for even suggesting it." He bristled as he moved about his kitchen, wiping down everything meticulously and replacing every spice he'd used back to exactly where he'd gotten it. I watched silently as he washed every dish by hand, then dried it before placing it back exactly where it belonged. Then, when he was done, he washed and dried his hands thoroughly before it seemed like he was more in control of himself.

"Cade," I spoke softly as I stood and came around the island to where he was standing, his hands braced on the counter and his head bowed. He didn't acknowledge me, too lost in the darkness of his thoughts to respond.

"Cade," My hands touched his lower back and his muscles flinched, but then relaxed as I slowly encircled his waist, pressing my cheek to his back. "I'm not going to let him send you back there, Cade. I promise. As long as we are together, we can take him. He won't win this time."

For a moment, he didn't respond, but then he turned and pulled me tight to his chest. His head bent and he buried his nose in my hair, breathing in my scent. "You don't get it, Juniper." He murmured against my hair. "I'm not worried about going back to prison."

I pulled back and looked up at him. "What do you mean?"

"Do you know what the hardest part about being locked up is?" The gold in his hazel eyes glinted in the dim light of the kitchen as he looked down at me. "It's all the time you have to think. I spent every day in that prison thinking about you, Juniper. If I wasn't hating you and raging against you, I was wondering what you were doing, where you were, who you were with." He gripped my chin in his hand, his thumb gently grazing the fullness of my bottom lip.

"I can go back to prison. But I can't go back to not having you in my life."

I swallowed the ache that his words caused.

"So you'd keep me in a prison instead?" I asked. He flinched and frowned at my words.

"What? No. Keeping you safe is not the same as keeping you in a prison." He said, as I pulled away from his embrace and shook my head at his denial.

"But it is, Cade. Don't you see? You want to keep me locked away to protect *you*." I folded my arms over my chest. "Do you think I want to put myself out there and risk my life? No. I don't. But I don't have a *choice*. Edmund wants *me*. These crazy, masked people want *me*. And I don't know why, believe me, I certainly didn't ask for it. But my mother gave up her life trying to make a better life for me. My father, Kage's dad, was *murdered* because of *me*." I said, with emotion riding every word. I was shaking, rage and anguish churning through me like a maelstrom, as all the thoughts I'd been consumed with over the past several days bubbled to the surface. "Stacy was taken because of *me*. And even you, Cade, you were imprisoned and locked away because of *me*. I am not running and hiding away anymore." My jaw clenched as I stood in his kitchen, watching his stony facade, hoping for a hint or a sign of any emotion other than the heated stare he gave me. "I came here to ask for your help, not your permission, Cade. Either you stand with me, or you can get the fuck out of my way."

He studied me for a few heartbeats of a moment before he shook his head with a resigned smirk, curling the corner of his lips and twisting the scar I'd grown to find one of the sexiest things on him. "Well, I tried. Fucking hell, I owe him a hundred bills now."

"What?" His quick emotional change had me feeling like I'd just been hit with whiplash, and while it sparked hope, it also confused the hell out of me. "Owe *who* a hundred?" I asked, shifting nervously on my bare feet.

He reached out to grab me, pulling me towards him as he gripped my chin and absently tucked a stray strand of hair behind my ear. "Your brother. Seems he knows you better than I realized. He said you'd never go for it, but I had to try."

I smacked his chest and glared. "Are you serious? Did you just try to guilt me into letting you lock me up? That's fucking manipulative as hell, Cade Black!" I wanted to be angry, but it was hard when his lips were teasing the sensitive flesh on my neck. He pulled back with a dark chuckle, but there was no hint of apology or remorse in his gaze.

"Let me be clear, pretty girl. I will do whatever it takes

to keep you safe. I will lie." His lips brushed against mine, and goosebumps danced along my flesh. "I will manipulate. I will murder. I will maim." He punctuated each statement with a soft kiss, his teeth gripping the edge of my lip and biting down gently as he pulled away, leaving me arching into him for more. "I agree that the only way to end this is to get Edmund out in the open, and you're our best option to do that. But don't think for one second that if I feel like you are too much at risk, I won't throw you over my shoulder and get you the fuck out of there. Do you understand me, Juniper? I will not take that chance."

His hands dipped under the shirt I was wearing, drawing it up around my hips and exposing that I was completely naked underneath. I gasped when his fingers danced along the edge of my folds, teasing at my opening, and I parted my thighs enough to let him slide his hand between them. "How many times do I have to tell you, Cade, you don't own me. You can't just tell me what to do all the time, and think I'll actually listen."

He picked me up unceremoniously and set me on the kitchen island behind me, where he spread my legs and knelt between them. His hooded eyes burned a dark gold as he looked up at me between my thighs. "Wrong, pretty girl. I own your body, heart and soul. Now lay back and let me remind you, why." And then his tongue touched my center and sparks exploded behind my eyes.

24

JUNIPER

I watched the long line of people that waited on the other side of a red velvet rope in the cold Denver air from the recesses of Kage's blacked-out Mercedes G-Wagon. They shivered in their tiny club dresses and sky-high heels as they waited for the bouncer to check IDs and usher them inside one of the city's most exclusive nightclubs.

Club Eros was located in one of the wealthiest districts of Denver, and only the who's who of the elite had access to its inner chambers.

The hopeful attendees who weren't part of this elite crowd put on their skimpiest, shiniest ensembles, and prayed that they made it to the front of the line where the bouncer would determine whether they met the night's requirements to pass beyond the velvet rope and inside.

No one knew ahead of time what the owner of the club would demand as the dress code for the evening. You had to guess and show up hoping that your chosen look for the evening earned you the right to be one of the chosen few.

On some nights, it was typical club fashion wear, with sequins and glitter being the only requirement. Other nights, they had to have certain physical features. Blondes would be passed over in favor of brunettes or redheads. Tall girls vs. short. There were never any men standing in the line. It was pretty much an unspoken rule that men were by invite only and had to be a part of the elite crowd, or be vouched for by someone who was already an attendee. Men could obviously show up and wait in line, but they were almost immediately rejected and told the club was at capacity.

There'd only been one time I'd heard of them announcing the dress code before opening the doors, and only because Stacy had gushed about it. It was a costume theme for Halloween. Once that had gotten out, there had been a raid on the local costume supply stores where hopeful attendees had nearly caused riots as they fought over costumes and sizes since there wasn't enough time to order anything. Police had to be called in and stores issued entry tickets to those who lined up to try their luck obtaining any kind of costume. Only for the bouncers to reject everyone that wasn't dressed like a pirate.

And somehow, my brother expected that we'd be able to waltz right up to those gilded doors and walk inside. I shifted on the soft leather and tugged at the neckline of my gown, nervous sweat already making my skin feel sticky in the climate-controlled interior. It felt like my makeup was sliding off my face, and I hadn't even made it through the doors yet.

"Ready?" Kage's smooth voice reached my ears, and I turned to see his dark eyes watching me intently from the shadows of the dimly lit interior. I shook my head and glanced back out at the club, and the line of hopefuls waiting for their turn.

"No." I frowned. "I'd honestly rather be back at the Pit after a fight night than doing this right now."

His lips twisted in a smirk as a sharply dressed valet attendant opened his door. Exiting the vehicle, he casually slipped a wad of bills into the attendant's hand before he opened my door to help me step out onto the sidewalk. "Honestly, I'd rather have you working the Pit after fight night as well. You don't want to know the money I've lost since you quit."

"Oh, really? Are you saying you'd hire me back?" The cold Colorado night air hit my skin, and I immediately regretted giving in to Kage's demand that I leave my leather jacket back at the hotel room. Apparently, the theme for the night was "Old Hollywood" and a leather jacket with more patches than leather wouldn't fit the vibe, or match the red velvet dress that clung to my hips and curves like a second skin. It had a sweetheart neckline and a tucked-in bodice that when paired with my hair, coiled and coiffed in loose waves, and my lips painted the same blood-red as the gown, I looked like I'd just stepped onto the red carpet of a new Cary Grant or Marilyn Monroe film. When I'd asked how he'd learned that piece of heavily guarded information, he'd only smirked and told me I wasn't ready to know all his secrets yet.

He laughed and took my elbow, pulling me in closer to him and the scent of his cologne, something dark and peppery hit my senses. Did our father used to wear the same cologne? "Not likely. I don't hire people that quit on me."

I scoffed, as I allowed him to lead me across the street toward the glittering throng of people. "You're just upset I hid in plain sight and got the slip on you."

Something dark flashed in those dangerous eyes as he cast a sidelong glance in my direction causing my skin to pebble, and not from the cold. It was moments like this that reminded me how very different my brother and I were. "Yes. It's not very often that the people I'm hunting stay out of my grasp for so long." He murmured. I wanted to ask him what he meant by that, but then we were approaching the trio of bouncers at the door and it was time to put the first part of Kage's plan into play. Two of the men were stationed on either side of the large doors, with arms crossed across thick, muscled chests. Their black suits were nearly bursting at the seams, and I wondered for a moment if they had to have them specially tailored. They looked like they were almost as expensive as the one Kage was wearing. The third guy was standing off to the side slightly, holding a clipboard. He was thinner and shorter than the other two by several inches, but gave off the air of being the one in charge, and he took his job way too seriously.

It was the shorter guy that Kage led me to.

The head bouncer eyed Kage with a flat, slightly bored expression as he looked at him and then down at the clipboard in his hand. I could have been a piece of lint on his arm for all the attention he directed at me. "Name?"

"Kage Diovolo." My brother stated, and at the sound of his name there were several gasps from the women who were crowding the velvet rope. The bouncer frowned and scrolled down the list before looking up at my brother.

"I'm sorry, Mr. Diovolo, I don't have you on the list for tonight."

Kage cocked his head, his lips spreading into a thin smile. It was like the surrounding air became colder in that moment, and I shifted closer to him, wishing that Cade was here instead. "Check again." He purred, but there was nothing soft about his tone.

The bouncer shifted but didn't look away, and I was slightly impressed by the man's nerves. "Mr. Diovolo, I'm sorry but tonight is list only as you know, and you aren't on it. Unless you have a sponsor for the evening, I'm afraid I can't allow you in."

Kage took one step toward the man and my pulse fluttered anxiously. A glance at the other bouncers told me they'd determined that Kage was a threat and were moving away from the door. Danger radiating from them. "I know very well what tonight is, and I'm telling you right now. *Check the list again.* Unless you want to have to explain to your boss why his personal guests were turned away at the door?"

The poor bouncer's mouth snapped shut. "Fine. Wait here." He turned to one of his counterparts and whispered something in his ear before he disappeared inside the double doors.

I leaned into Kage and murmured softly. "Personal guests of the boss? Who is that?"

"You'll see. Just follow my lead." He kept his gaze trained on the doors while I anxiously turned all the scenarios over in my head. Our plan hinged on being one step ahead of both Edmund and the Infernals. And to do that, we had to approach them on neutral ground. This club was apparently frequented by someone high up in the secretive organization. Our plan was to get inside, get an audience with this person and convince them to help us.

I did not know if it would work or not, but Kage was convinced that he could persuade this person that it was in their best interest to help us. But only if we could get inside. Where was the snobby bouncer dude?

I shifted and rubbed my arms briskly. "How is it you run in these circles but don't have a membership to this place?" I asked.

He chuckled. "I'm so glad you think so highly of me already, my dear sister, but I'm afraid there are some circles that aren't yet open to me."

"Yet?" I looked down at my feet, clad in strappy gold heels, and I counted each toe as they went numb one by one. If that bouncer didn't get back soon, I was going to kick him in the balls with my frozen toes.

"Yet." He repeated, as he pulled me closer to him while pulling off his overcoat and wrapping it around my shoulders. Immediately, I was enveloped in warmth and the scent of my brother. Familiarness sank into me and I stopped shivering. "But that's something I hope to remedy." His smile was warm. "With your help."

I frowned, pulling his coat tighter around me. I wanted

to ask him what he meant, but just then the head bouncer was back, and we both turned to look at him.

"The boss says you may come in, but you may not partake. You are to follow me and do exactly as I say. Do you understand?" There was no room for argument in his voice.

Kage nodded, a polite smile stretching across his face. I could tell that the bouncer's curt attitude wasn't settling well with him, but he was willing to go along with it in order to be allowed access inside. "Of course." His voice was a cultured purr. "Lead the way."

The bouncer turned sharply on his heel and lead us toward the entrance. Kage guided me along with him, his hand resting on the small of my back. I felt his breath and his low voice in my ear. "Stay close to me, Juniper. And no matter what you see inside, keep your mouth shut and let me do the talking." I nodded, unable to speak around the lump in my throat. What the hell kind of club was this? What did I get myself into?

25

JUNIPER

Darkness engulfed us as we stepped inside the atrium, broken only by a faint, red glow from the lights that cast an eerie ambiance on the sleek, black floor as we made our way towards the second set of doors. Next to them, a pair of bouncers loomed, one of which extended his hand, signaling us to stop once more.

"Mr. Diovolo, if you would be so kind as to hold out your arms." Kage cocked his head and turned to where the head bouncer had spoken just off to the side of us.

"I don't recall being searched the last time I attended an event here." Kage said to him.

"After the…" He paused and cleared his throat. "… *incident*, at the last event you attended, our boss thought it prudent to make sure you did not *accidentally* violate the rules of this establishment again."

"I see..." Kage drawled out, and I got the distinct impression that he was considering making an *incident* out of the bouncer right here, before we even entered the main portion of the club. The guy was grating on my brother's nerves, and mine. But Kage only turned back around and held out his arms in compliance. The bouncer who had stopped us stepped forward, starting to pat Kage down.

His counterpart cleared his throat and nodded in my direction, indicating that I should do the same. I huffed and shrugged out of my brother's overcoat, handing it to the man and then spread out my arms. "I seriously doubt you need to look too closely. There's not exactly a lot of room to hide anything in this dress."

The bouncer didn't say a word, but gave me an appreciative once over before stepping forward to trace his hands down my ribs towards the curve of my hips. I hissed out a breath when his hands wandered dangerously close to the exposed skin of my thigh, and Kage's voice growled low in the dim light. "Touch one inch of my sister's skin and you'll not have a single finger left to jerk-off with."

The man flinched, stepping back as the head bouncer stiffened next to us. "We weren't aware that you had a sister, Mr. Diovolo. We assumed you had brought one of your usual companions." The man spoke as if the information had changed the dynamics in the room.

"Well, I did not. And now that you know who she is, I would suggest that you treat her accordingly. She is not to be marked." Kage took his overcoat from the bouncer who was swallowing nervously in front of me, his eyes wide as they shifted nervously back and forth between Kage and his boss. After a brief pause, where it looked like the head guy was about to have a cranium implosion, he finally nodded. "Ms. Diovolo is exempt from the inspection. She may enter."

I shot Kage with a pointed glare. What the fuck had he not been telling me about this club? "Well, I feel like I just passed an exam I didn't know I needed to study for."

None of the other people in the room laughed or looked in my direction, and I leaned in to whisper to my brother. "Are you going to tell me what that was all about?"

He settled his hand protectively on my lower back once more, and guided me toward the doors now being opened by the bouncer. "Later." He murmured, then we were being ushered into another atrium that was larger and more brightly lit. As I approached, the distant sound of music grew louder, emanating from behind another set of doors and I could feel my nerves calming down for the first time since we entered the building. Despite the cryptic words and the creepy pat-downs by the bouncers, this was in fact just a normal nightclub, and for the first time since I'd agreed to this entire plot, I felt like I was in my element.

Two female attendants were waiting for us. They quietly came and collected Kage's overcoat, then asked if there was anything I'd like to check before we entered the main club. Kage gave them a curt, "No." and they skittered away with nervous glances back at the two of us, while I tried not to let his bossiness get under my skin.

As the third set of doors opened, the pulsating bass from inside the infamous Club Eros hit us like a wave. We stepped out onto a balcony supported by tall, Roman columns, and I gasped in amazement. It was like someone had taken an ancient colosseum and dropped it right in the middle of the Colorado mountains. And just below us —where the gladiators would have fought, bled and died, throngs of bodies were intertwining and grinding themselves on each other in a sweaty mess, to the beats of deep house music that reverberated off the walls.

The dance floor was flanked by an amphitheater on three sides, its tiered rows of seating and tables providing a perfect perch for partiers to gaze upon the chaos of bodies writhing to the music. Suspended from the ceiling in varying degrees of heights, were gilded cages filled with dancers clad in barely-there costumes from the ancient world. Some were nymphs or cupids, others were gladiators or goddesses. All of them exuded nothing but pure, sexual energy as they moved in time with the dark music that was pumping through the crowd.

My jaw dropped. I'd never seen anything like it in my life. And I'd seen a lot of crazy shit as a bartender at the Pit.

Kage grabbed my hand and pulled me along behind him as he started down the stairs. "Come on."

My jaw snapped shut, and I dug my heels in, forcing Kage to come to a complete stop atop one of the sets of stairs that would lead us down to the main dance floor. "No."

From where we remained halted on the balcony, the columns and heavily draped curtains dampened the music and the noise of the crowd. Kage turned to me with a frown, his dark eyes glittering in the dim lighting. "We don't have time for this, Juniper." I could hear the barely contained impatience in his voice. My brother didn't like the word 'No'. Too fucking bad.

"No." I repeated and stepped closer to him, the height difference now level between us as he stood just a few steps below me. "What we don't have time for, is cryptic games and you acting like I'm a piece of property you can speak and make decisions for. Tell me what the hell that inspection was about and why being your sister makes me exempt from it."

His jaw muscles pulsed with tension, those glittering dark pupils narrowing into menacing slits, as his gaze bore into mine. I couldn't see my reflection in them. "Nothing about this place or these people is what it seems, June." He growled through clenched teeth. "If I hadn't spoken up and claimed you as my blood, they would have inspected you, drugged you and then separated us. And I would have been utterly powerless to protect you." He hissed the words climbing up a step, elevating himself slightly. "The rules here are different, Juniper, and we have to play by them or they will become suspicious. So if that means I act like an overbearing asshole, it's because that's exactly what they expect me to be." He gripped my arm but his touch was gentle, even as he towered over me once more. "You need to trust me."

I swallowed, my gaze flickering around us as I suddenly noticed that we were being watched by a few waiters and waitresses who kept glancing up from the floor below us. Chills went up my spine, and I recalled Cade's warning before I'd left with my brother. *"Club Eros is not what it seems, and neither is your brother. But where you can trust Kage, you can't trust what you see at Eros. Keep close to Kage. He'll keep you safe until I can get there."*

. . .

I nodded, and Kage visibly relaxed then turned around and descended the steps once more as I dutifully followed behind him.

At the bottom of the steps, a pretty blonde woman in a glittering black gown approached us.

"Mr. Diovolo," she curtsied, her head bowed in graceful subservience. "We are delighted to have you this evening. Will you be remaining in the Asphodel room this evening? Or shall I prepare for your usual entertainment?"

"Neither." Kage cast a bored look around the room aptly named after a place in the Greek underworld where the minds of the dead were numbed. I wondered how many of the drugged and drunken bodies that were grinding against each other on the dance floor actually understood the double meaning. "We're here to see your master."

The girl's gaze snapped upwards for the briefest of seconds, her lips curling in a condescending smirk as she glanced between us, before she once again bowed her head in an apology that didn't quite feel sincere. "I'm sorry to disappoint you, Mr. Diovolo, but Master Salerno is not here this evening. I shall prepare a private suite for you and your guest in the meantime." She turned to go, dismissing us, but Kage snatched his hand out and grabbed her by the arm. This time there was nothing gentle with his grip and I could see her porcelain skin blanch where his fingers dug in tightly. "You will tell your master that I am here and that I would like an audience with him. I have a special guest with me who he would not want to miss meeting. Do you understand?"

I thought the girl would cry out in pain, but instead her lips turned down in a sultry pout and I swore I saw her eyes glaze over with lust for the briefest of moments. "Of course, Mr. Diovolo. My apologies for misunderstanding. If it pleases you, follow me."

My head felt like it was on a swivel as I looked back and forth between the woman and my brother. What the hell just happened? I wouldn't get any answers though, because Kage released her roughly and she quickly recovered, turning on a graceful heel before leading us away from the dance floor toward an almost invisible alcove near the main staircase.

Kage shortened his stride enough that I could catch up with him, and he leaned down to whisper in my ear. "Stay close and remember what I said." And then we disappeared behind thick, velvet curtains and I was once again plunged into darkness.

26

JUNIPER

The darkness didn't last long as a faint glow illuminated from a panel which the woman had placed her palm against, as a hidden door slid open silently, revealing a long corridor. The woman waved us through and the moment we stepped into the hall, the door slid closed once more behind us, and with it, the sounds of the club and party-goers behind us disappeared. It was as if Club Eros no longer existed, and I realized that anyone who might stick their curious heads through the curtains would not understand what the alcove was hiding.

We followed silently behind the nameless woman with only the sounds of our heels clicking on the tiled floor, echoing off the walls until we reached the end of the hall where an elevator awaited us. She pushed a button and stood back as the doors slid open, revealing a luxurious interior complete with gilded and mirrored paneling. Bowing once more, she spoke to Kade, not once looking at me. "Master Salerno is waiting for you. You are kindly asked to remember the rules of the Elysium, and not to stray from the path. Please enjoy your evening, Mr. Diovolo."

Then she pushed a button once more and the door closed, sealing us inside. I turned to Kage. "What the fuck is this place? I feel like I've stepped into the Twilight Zone." The elevator started its descent and my stomach dropped. Kage's face remained a stone façade.

"Just remember what I said and stick to the plan. When we get to Salerno's suite, let me do the talking. Cade should be in place by now if we need a quick way out. And for fuck's sake, Juniper..." He slid those glittering, obsidian orbs my way. "... whatever you do, don't stray from the path. No matter what you see."

I put my hands up defensively. "I got it, I got it! I know how to stick to a plan. Sheesh." Kage's brows furrowed further as he silently conveyed that somehow he didn't believe me, but I ignored him because in that instant, the elevator came to a slow stop. We both turned to face the doors and my gasp of shock was audible. Whatever I'd mentally prepared myself to expect to see, it was nothing compared to the scene that was laid out before me.

I suddenly understood why this place was called the Elysium. Because like the Greek underworld it was named after, the giant room we entered was crafted to look like something straight out of the myths. Lush carpets of grass and vibrant flowers filled the room. Trees—actual trees with roots going down into the earth, filled the chamber. Birds chirped sweetly as they flew from tree to tree, while butterflies flitted from flower to flower.

A path led from the elevator through the rolling fields, and I stumbled as we stepped out onto it, with Kage quickly reaching out to catch my arm and steady me.

"When I first came here, it wasn't called *Elysium*." He murmured as he began to lead me along the path. "They'd modeled it after Tartarus that night. And instead of flowers and trees, there were pits of boiling lava, and I'm pretty sure blood."

"You mean they brought all of this down here for just one night?" I gaped in disbelief. "Who the hell are these people?"

"Maybe not one night. I haven't quite figured out if it's on a schedule or if it's purely by whim, but they change up the scene every so often. As for who? Very rich, very bored, very dangerous people who want to believe they can achieve godhood just by roleplaying it."

"You mean like the Infernals?" We continued down the path, but movement out of the corner of my eye caught my attention. I craned my head to look, and in that moment I realized that not everything in the room was real. We were in-fact in a room that couldn't have been much larger than a ballroom, but well placed screens with images projected onto them made it seem much bigger. The details were so grand and well done that I was sure that anyone drugged, or drunk enough to stumble up here would have a hard time determining illusion from reality.

"No. Not the Infernals, although some of their group frequent this place." Kage continued along, lecturing as he went. "They call the main club area the Asphodel, and keep it restricted to the common people, but this area…" He waved a hand to encompass our surroundings. "…is the land of the gods. Occasionally they will bring someone who catches their eye into their realm and *elevate* them."

"Is that what they were going to do to me?" A flash of white amongst the green had me slowing down to process whatever it was I was seeing. Was that a *satyr*? I blinked, thinking that the scenery and Kage's explanation were giving me hallucinations. Another flash of fur and a bare chest smacked the reality back into me. Nope. That was indeed a man dressed up as a satyr. Complete with the horns, lute, and several half-naked women writhing on the surrounding ground.

A low moan reached my ears, and I whipped my head back around to stare at the path directly ahead of me.

Correction, those totally naked women writhing on the ground *with him*.

"No," Kage answered. "They thought you were a sacrifice."

"A what?!" My shriek had Kage turning to look back at me with a disapproving frown.

"What the hell do you mean by *sacrifice*?" I hissed, quieter now, hoping that the fake satyr sandwich on the hill next to us had not been disturbed by my outburst.

Kage cleared his throat. "It doesn't matter. They know you aren't to be touched." He spoke as if by his will alone, he could make that statement a reality.

"Okay, but it *does* matter, brother dear. What if they decide I'm a good sacrifice anyway and don't care that I'm your sister? And why did they think *you* were bringing someone to them, anyway?" It was at that precise moment when we made a sharp turn that I realized—we were gradually nearing a grand, white canvas tent that had been expertly assembled right in the center of the fake field.

"They won't touch you, so stop worrying. And it's because the last time I was here, I stole their selected sacrifice." He stopped a few feet from the tent and glared at me as if he was annoyed that he'd revealed that much to me.

I cocked a brow. "You mean *the incident?*" I said, mimicking the bouncer from earlier.

He said nothing, but shot me a warning look before striding forward and entering the tent. I had no choice but to follow behind him.

Another scene greeted us, once more mimicking Greek mythology and what I assumed was supposed to represent the heavens. Half-dressed women and men lounged around on silken cushions talking and laughing, while others congregated on a small dance floor. To the back of the tent was a raised platform with a large gilded, ornate couch on it. Behind that was a wall of one-way windows that looked down upon the main club below.

Now I knew why the ceiling was painted like it was. We were literally in the heavens while the writhing crowd languished in euphoria below us.

Kage came to a stop before the couch and I got a good look at the man who sprawled across it. Dressed in a golden toga revealing a broad chest above a barrel belly, was a heavy set man with a crown of laurel leaves resting on his salt and pepper head. Two women—wearing strips of cloth that someone might call dresses, except that they were so sheer that I could make out every inch of their naked bodies— were draped across him. Their hands wandered over his hairy chest in a slow and languid way that made me take a closer look at their too-made-up faces and glossy eyes. They were probably not even old enough to legally drink, and appeared to be heavily drugged. Bile rose in the back of my throat. The lounge he was occupying dipped under his weight, the gold legs bowed outward from the strain. This had to be Salerno.

Beady eyes narrowed at Kage as a sardonic grin split his lips revealing too-white teeth. "Mr. Diavolo, I must say I'm surprised to see you here again, given the last time you joined the festivities. I believe I told you never to come back. I wasn't under the impression that you had a death wish." There was a biting edge to his voice that betrayed the smile. Salerno wasn't happy to see Kage at all, and I had a sinking feeling that we were already starting off on a bad foot. Whatever Kage had done the last time he'd been here, whatever sacrifice he'd stolen, Salerno wasn't going to let it go so easily. I swallowed past the lump in my throat. We had to convince Salerno to help us. I had to save Stacy.

"I don't. I'm here as an ambassador of good will. And I come with an offer for you." Kage's voice was dark and smooth as he stared down Salerno, his dark gaze never blinking.

Salerno leaned forward, his eyes burning brightly as they flickered in my direction, and I saw something slither in their depths that made my skin crawl. "Ahhh..." His head cocked toward me, predator-like and assessing as his gaze traveled up and down my body, not even bothering to hide as he lingered over the swell of my breasts and the exposed skin of my legs. "You've brought me a new offering. And a tempting one at that." His gaze swiveled back to Kage. "But I'm afraid simply replacing one sacrifice with another isn't how it's done. You stole from me, Kage Diovolo. Do you have any idea what the repercussions were because of your insolence?" He licked his lips and turned his gaze back toward me once more. "Sampling the goods, before accepting your peace offering, would convince me to overlook the slight."

Kage's jaw muscles flexed just once, and I knew that only our mission here prevented him from pulverizing the fat pervert and splattering his guts across the chaise that Salerno was sprawled across.

"I think you have a bad habit of misunderstanding situations, Master Salerno. Exactly the way you misunderstood what was happening the last time I was here." The way he drawled out "Master" left no doubt that he didn't consider the man a *master* of anything, other than stupidity perhaps. "I'm not here to offer that kind of offering, or any other type of offering to you ever again."

Salerno's gaze snapped back to Kage's with a glare and a lip curled in disdain. "Then it appears you have a death wish, after all. Pity. I was hoping you'd see the error of your ways once you tired of that little devil's pussy. Tell me, where is the girl now? Getting passed around like a Sunday dinner with your Diablos? Or did you actually think you could tame the whore and make her respectable?"

I thought Kage would snap. I had no idea who this girl was that Salerno was referring to, but it didn't take much to guess that it was the sacrifice my brother had stolen away and apparently forfeited his membership into this club for. 'She-devil', he'd called her. A whore. I spared a glance at Kage wondering who this woman was that he'd set aside his ruthless nature to safeguard.

Kage's voice dripped pure venom, a contrast to the hardened, emotionless mask of his face. "The only death on the table is yours, Salerno. You just haven't realized it yet."

I gasped as a shadow peeled away from the wall and approached Salerno from behind. A soft *click*, barely audible under the sound of music from the dance floor, sent a chill across my skin.

I saw the glint of the barrel first, then my eyes flew upward to the figure, who cast a lazy wink in my direction and my heart fluttered. Cade.

27

JUNIPER

$\mathcal{S}$alerno paled, a thin sheen of sweat breaking out across his forehead. "What's the meaning of this, Kage?" His voice was less sure, less arrogant-sounding with the barrel of a gun pressed to his temple. The music stopped as an eerie silence descended over the room, even as the pulsing beat from the nightclub below us reverberated through the floor beneath my feet. The girls who had draped themselves like human blankets across Salerno's wide body slunk away like wraiths, their glazed expressions never changing even though they knew that their master's life hung by a thin thread. I watched as one of them turned a barely conscious gaze to Cade and nodded—just slightly, before slipping behind the same curtained wall he'd appeared from.

So that's how he'd gotten in.

"Club Eros is officially under new management, Salerno." It was Cade who answered, not Kage, and my eyes widened slightly at the edge I heard to his clipped words. This was a side of Cade I'd never seen before. Behind us, I could hear the shuffling of feet as the people who'd been in attendance were allowed to slip away. Not one patron said a word in protest. Not a single person stepped up to defend their so-called master. Something that Salerno seemed to have just realized as he cast his gaze around in a panic, searching for the bouncers who'd plagued us not twenty minutes prior.

When he finally realized that it was just the four of us alone in the private sanctuary, he snarled, his face turning purple as rage settled over his features. "You bastard, you think you can bring your dog in here and intimidate me into letting you into my club? You're dead, Kage. You'll never walk out of here alive."

I expected Kage to respond, but it was Cade who came around to stand in front of the both of us, his gun still pressed to Salerno's temple. "Pretty sure you're the one who's not walking away from this situation, Sal. I told you the next time a girl showed up on my doorstep claiming she'd been 'chosen' by you or one of your club members, we were going to have a little conversation about it. And it's no longer your club. It's mine."

My eyes grew wide at the revelation. Cade owned

Club Eros now? How on earth had he managed that? I knew Cade had money, but this was next-level wealth that I'd never expected him to possess.

Something flickered across Kage's face—surprise? Before he masked it and smoothly said, "As I said before, Salerno, I came as an ambassador of goodwill. Not *my* goodwill—" He tipped his head toward Cade. "—but his. You crossed the line, Sal," he said, using Cade's nickname for him. "Not once, but twice. And now it's time to pay the piper."

"What do you want?" Salerno snarled, his defiant tone dripping venom despite the realization that no one would come to his rescue. Cade's smile was pure malevolence that sent chills down my spine. "—I want nothing," he calmly responded, pausing after each word, his tone carrying a sense of sinister intent. "But she—" he gave a barely perceptible nod in my direction. "...has a use for you, and that's the only thing keeping you alive right now."

Sal's body twisted toward me, a look of disgusted disbelief flashing across his features as he reevaluated me under the new light of this information. "And who is *she?*"

"She—" Kage started, but I stepped forward, tired of hearing men speak as if I was nothing more than a prop in their power dynamics.

"*She* can speak for herself." I said calmly, as Cade

moved aside just slightly to give me room to stand directly in front of Salerno, but still just out of his reach. "I'm Juniper Wild, Mr. Salerno. I believe you know my father."

Salerno snorted. "The only Edmund Wild I know is six feet under rotting in a grave he dug himself."

I shook my head softly. "I'm afraid your information is out of date, Mr. Salerno. Edmund is very much alive, and I need to know how to find him."

Those beady eyes widened before narrowing just slightly, and I could see the wheels turning in his mind. He was taking in this information and calculating how to best use it to his advantage. "I'm not sure what makes you think I could help. Edmund is a snake. If he faked his death and slithered off to hide somewhere, you're better off leaving him there to rot or leech off someone else." He leaned forward and gave me a closer inspection. "Wait, did you say he was your father? I wasn't aware that Edmund had any children."

"He's not my biological father." I didn't bother to elaborate or mention my younger brother. The fewer people who knew about Dean and his relation to Edmund or myself, the better. But it was interesting to hear that someone who had intimate knowledge of the Infernals and Edmund Wild would think he was childless. I fought the urge to question him about it. Right now, my focus was finding out where Edmund might have taken Stacy.

"Ahh…" He sat back and flicked a glance at Cade, who'd no longer had his gun trained on him, but still crowded his space. His aura was a dark and menacing presence that told me he didn't need a weapon to intimidate Salerno if he proved to be uncooperative. "And what's in it for me if I cooperate?"

"You get to live, for one." I held up a finger, annoyed that despite the threat from both Cade and Kage at my side, this man was still arrogant enough to think he could make a deal. "Second, you get to live with all your *extremities* intact." I dropped my gaze pointedly to his crotch as I raised a second finger. "And lastly, you'll be allowed to continue your private parties here with a few amendments to the rules." Kage and Cade both whipped their heads toward me at that last statement, and I shrugged a half-hearted apology for butting into their territory. "Since I'm sure it's good for business." I added, sarcasm twisting my lips into a half-hearted smile.

Salerno studied me for a moment before giving a nod. "Fine, although I still don't know how you expect me to be able to help you. Edmund and I aren't exactly friendly with each other, and I certainly never sought him out willingly."

"But you know how to find him if you need to, don't you? You both have the same connections. You run in the same circles."

He snorted and curled his lips in disgust. "Edmund *wishes* he ran in the same circles as I do. He was always sniffing around the edges like a coyote looking for carrion. Once, he got close…close enough to taste what it was like. But then he was rejected, and he spent the rest of his miserable life trying to gain access again. I heard he'd aligned himself with some lower-level crime bosses to replace what he'd lost. But of course," He leaned forward, his eyes gleaming and full of power-lust. "…once you taste ambrosia, nothing else can compare."

The Infernals. That had to be what Salerno was talking about, but I needed to be sure. "Let's say I wanted to taste this *ambrosia* for myself. What would I need to do?"

A single bushy eyebrow raised a bit, while he shook his head in response. "I'm afraid there's no way for someone like you to do that. You see, these circles have a hierarchy. Membership in the order is limited to those who are born into it, or those who pass a highly stringent selection process. Sadly, you don't have the correct last name, nor does your anatomy allow you to be considered as a candidate for their selection."

"You mean it's a boys only club?" My thoughts immediately flew to the polaroid I'd found with Edmund, my mother, father and David all wearing the strange masks. Had they all been vying for entry into the Infernals? All but my mother, of course. It was hers by birthright, according to Kage.

"No. But the women have a role to play just as the men do. I've already said too much," He grumbled, adjusting the front of his toga as if just now realizing how exposed he was to me, to us. "If you want to find Edmund, I'd suggest starting with some of the low-level thugs he hung out with."

"You've said just enough, Mr. Salerno." I forced a tight smile as his brows furrowed in confusion. "Because now I know exactly how you can help me."

It was a dangerous game we were playing now. And it all rested on trusting Kage to know what he was doing and who we were dealing with. "You're going to introduce me to this *order* that you speak of, and then you're going to help me track down any connections that Edmund might have."

"I already told you!" He stammered. "There's no way to gain entrance unless—" I cut him off. "Except through life and death. Unless you complete the circle. Well, guess what, Mr. Salerno? I am the circle. I can either be your life or I can be your death. Which do you choose?"

My words hung in the air like daggers, poised to slice and cut. To make him bleed. They were the words I'd remember Jax screaming as he was dying by Kage's hands and, as Salerno had spoken, I suddenly knew what they had meant. What my mother's words in her diary had meant. His eyes grew wide. The jowls of Salerno's cheeks shook as he gaped at me—in shock and recognition. "My god. I should have seen it. You look just like her…I just, we thought…my god." He repeated, and then suddenly he was kneeling, his thick body sliding off the lounge until he was on the floor at my feet.

"The Heir. The Heir has returned."

"So it seems she has." A deep, raspy voice that I hadn't heard in a long, long time came from the doorway behind us, and all of our heads whipped in the speaker's direction.

Nothing could have prepared me for the punch-to-the-gut feeling I got when I saw who was standing there, his thin frame lit by the glow of fake sunlight coming from the room beyond. "You're— dead…" I breathed on an exhale.

"Not quite as dead as some would like me to be, Juniper." There was a sorrowfulness in his tone, even as he said it in jest. Then hazel-green eyes turned to Cade, and I turned along with him to see Cade's face—frozen in a mix of stunned and silent rage. "Hello, son." David Black acknowledged.

AFTERWORD

Ok, who needs a bandaid? A hug? Maybe you want to write me a love letter telling me how much you loved it and can't wait for the next one? I'm kidding about the bandaid and hug part, but I do love to hear from readers. Please be sure to email me authoranneroman@gmail.com

And please, reviews are so helpful to authors, even if you hated it although I hope you didn't and in that case I will probably be the one who needs a hug. So leave that review and be sure to join my mailing list at www.annero manauthor.com to find out when Cade & Juniper's story will be continuing. Because I might like to drop you off the edge of a cliff from time to time, but I'll NEVER leave you hanging. Xoxo- Anne

Did you enjoy the book? Consider purchasing the entire e-book to own. Kindle Unlimited is a fantastic resource for readers and authors alike but only permits the author to earn royalties off of one read-through. Your support helps authors like me continue to write and do what we love. Thank you so much for reading!

ACKNOWLEDGMENTS

I can't leave without acknowledging the people that made this book happen.

To my husband. My real-life book boyfriend, best friend, and muse. I love you. Thank you for knowing me so well and understanding how much peace writing brings to me. To my kids and family. Thank you for letting me write when I said I needed to get words in and for being so patient with me. I love you and I'm so thankful to you.

To my Muffins. You know who you are. Thank you for always being ready to garden, read, laugh, and encourage me in everything. I love you all so much.

To my author friends and mentors, Amelia and Debbie, I couldn't do it without you. Thank you so much for all your guidance and advice.

To my beta readers and my beautiful editor Mandy. You guys really made this book come together. Thank you for being patient with me through all the changes and updates and rewrites. You're brilliant and I'm so thankful for you.

And to my readers. I hope I spark even just a moment of joy with every book I write in someone, and if that someone is you, I'm so thankful for you. Xoxo- Anne

ABOUT THE AUTHOR

Anne Roman is the author of suspenseful, 'edge of your seat' romance. She loves to write exciting twists and turns that leave her readers begging for more. When not writing you can find Anne playing Uber driver to one of her four children, hanging out with her hunky husband, or catering to two very spoiled cats and one spoiled dog. Want to get to know her? Join her Facebook group here:

Anne Roman- Romance on the Edge